CW01561691

AN AMISH EXTRAORDINARY LOVE

EMMA CARTWRIGHT

This is a work of fiction. Any names or characters, businesses or places, events or incidents, are fictitious. Any resemblance to actual persons, living or dead, or actual events is purely coincidental.

CHAPTER 1

*T*his is aptly named, Helena Berry thought with a hint of sarcasm, her gray eyes taking in the remnants of her uncle's dilapidated farmhouse on the outskirts of Holmes County. Nothing about it seemed to be in working order, despite the fact nothing was particularly in need of fixing, either. Broken Wheel indeed.

Her high heels clicked on the faded wooden floors as the real estate agent in front babbled on about the wainscoting and arched ceilings, his voice pouring on and on about the virtues of the home but Helena's mind was on other matters as she paused by the filthy living room windows to peer out at the cornfields, now abandoned by the workers for the day —possibly for good now that her uncle wasn't returning to oversee their labor. She hadn't decided entirely what to do with them yet, given that she had no idea what she was in for with this monstrosity she had inherited. She felt a stab of guilt at having to let them go but maintaining a farm simply wasn't in the cards while her work was in the city, charming as the idea was on paper. And the scan she'd done of her uncle's numbers told her that this place wasn't going to sustain itself.

She had entertained the notion at first, when the estate lawyer had presented the paperwork, but the more she thought about it, the more Helena recognized that it simply was impossible. Helena had too full a life in Akron already and even without an in-depth look at the numbers, she could tell that the farm was barely pulling in a profit. Under the guidance of someone without experience, it was certain to fail, even with trained hands working.

What was Uncle Clyde thinking, leaving this place to me?

Another piercing of emotion overtook Helena as she realized her uncle had no one else to leave the house to, his niece the only living relative left to tend to his estate—if that's what this could be called. It also made sense that Clyde knew his numbers-sensible niece would do the best thing and sell the property, while he had probably been too attached to it for too many years to do the same.

He wants me to get rid of it. It's the only cause of action that makes sense.

"How long will it take to sell?" Helena interrupted the chatty agent, cutting him off mid-sentence. If she hadn't, she wouldn't have gotten a word in edge wise, she was certain. He had barely stopped speaking since entering the house almost half an hour earlier.

Cory Jameson was his name, and he was apparently the "best in Broken Wheel" according to his advertisement online. Helena suspected that the bar wasn't very high in a town of less than five thousand. Perched on the outskirts of Holmes County, Broken Wheel was barely a blip on any map, anyway. Cory Jameson was likely one of two agents in the entire town. She had not looked very hard for an agent, her desire to be done with the sale outweighing her need for the perfect real estate broker. There wasn't any time to sit around in the boondocks and write out pros and cons lists. The sooner this was done, the sooner she could get home.

"Are you sure you want to sell?" Cory asked again, his drawling voice beginning to grind on Helena's nerves. "This property has good bones, despite what you see and the land—"

"Mr. Jameson, I'm an accountant, not a farmer," Helena interjected for a second time. "And isn't this Amish country?"

He appeared taken aback by her question. "Well, yes, predominately...but there are lots of Englisch farmers here—that's what the Amish call us—Englisch. Your uncle ran his farm among them without any incident. They don't bother the Englischers and do trade with them. You could do the same just as so many other Englisch have done—"

Helena didn't care for a history lesson on Amish relations. That wasn't why she'd asked the question. "Would any of the Amish be interested in purchasing this house, since it's so close to their lands, anyway?"

The gangly salesman shifted his weight uncomfortably and ambled closer. "Possibly. The house would have to be refitted without electricity, I imagine. There are some other issues that would make it uninhabitable for the Amish, but it could be worked around. This Order is very conservative. Others are less so but—"

Cory was off on another tangent, which Helena tuned out, her mind on six other matters, none of which pertained to the house itself or the Amish who lived nearby.

She had clients waiting for her and she was losing a day of work by being there. She was sure her bosses at the accounting firm were displeased with her, upsetting their schedule with this unplanned leave of absence, and she didn't like being away from home.

"What will you do about the cattle?" The query drew her back to the living room where she stood. Her head cocked, and she gawked at him, sure she'd misheard.

"The *what?*" she sputtered, blinking as she spun around. The estate lawyer had made no mention of any cows during the reading of the will.

"Oh…there's a herd of cattle," Cory explained, nodding. He waved a hand as if he intended to show her, but Helena made no effort to move. She didn't need to get her expensive heels dirty. "That's how your uncle made his living, I understand."

"Of course, there is," Helena groaned, hanging her head, wondering what other surprises she might expect. "What am I supposed to do with the cattle?"

"I'm sure I can find buyers for the livestock if you're sure about selling, but it will take time. Most of the farmers in these parts are properly outfitted."

"How much time?" Helena sighed. Time was not something she had, but she suspected that telling Cory Jameson this would get her nowhere.

"That I can't say, Mrs. Berry. It takes as long as it takes. People around here don't move as fast as they do in the city."

"*Ms.* Berry," Helena bristled, and Cory bowed his head.

"Of course. But that doesn't change the fact that I can't rush things."

She gritted her teeth.

"Fine," Helena agreed quickly. "Find buyers for the cattle and the land. The sooner you can get this done, the better."

She considered offering him more money for his troubles, but she stopped short. She wasn't sure she liked him enough for that yet. The last thing she needed was him doing a half job under the promise of extra cash.

Biting on her lower lip, Helena showed the agent to the door, her mind reeling.

"Are you heading back to Akron?" he asked, but she shook her head, making the decision on the spot.

"There's internet here, right?" she asked slowly, dreading the answer. She didn't want to imagine what it might take to set it up, even for a week or two.

It'll take two weeks just to set up the internet all the way out here!

A cold sweat broke out over Helena's forehead.

"I imagine so," Cory replied. "Your uncle appeared to have all the modern luxuries."

Helena glanced at the unfinished wood floor and ancient furniture without comment. It was leaps and bounds from her pristine condo in the city. She would hardly call this "modern luxury."

"I'll find the password and stay a few days," she said, moderately relieved to hear of one less problem. "But please, work quickly. I really need to get back to the city."

"I'll do my best," he promised, offering her a wide smile as he stepped over the threshold.

You'd better. Your commission depends on it, she stopped herself from reminding him.

"You have my number," Helena told him stiffly.

The door closed behind him and Helena released a breath she hadn't known she'd been holding as she spun around to stare at the interior of the house again.

Oh, Uncle Clyde. Why did you leave this on my shoulders?

As if to answer her question, a low rumble of thunder echoed in the distance and Helena rolled her eyes skyward.

She hadn't seen her uncle in years before his funeral, her father's brother an elusive, solitary soul who had disappeared into the country not long after Helena's parents had passed in a car accident. Helena had not made much of an effort to reach out to him either, assuming the man wanted to be left in peace, which made the call from the lawyer all the more surprising, two weeks earlier.

Is this my penance for not having kept in touch?

Another grumble of distant thunder appeared to mock her, but the buzz of her cell phone in her pocket distracted Helena from any further self-pity. Flipping her dark red hair away from her face, she answered Melissa's call on the second ring.

"How's it going out in the boonies?" her friend asked with a short laugh. "Did you catch diphtheria yet?"

Helena chuckled mirthlessly. "About as well as can be expected, I guess. The man has cows. Cows, Lissa!"

"I'm not surprised," Melissa snorted. "Does he have chickens, too?"

A crack of lightning caused Helena to jump, and she hurried across the foyer to close the windows as rain began to splatter against the open panes. "Geez!"

"What's that noise?" Melissa asked in alarm.

"I think a storm's coming in," Helena breathed, her pulse quickening. She chuckled, amused by her own nerves.

"Are you coming back tonight? There are a few new clients you should see," Melissa warned as Helena continued to shut the open windows, securing herself in the big, drafty house. "And you know how the bosses are."

Helena swallowed a groan at the reminder.

"No." She sighed unhappily. "I'm going to stay until matters are settled here. Email me whatever you need and I'll work remotely for now. If it becomes an issue, I'll go back and forth."

"That sounds like a real pain."

"Hopefully, the house and livestock will be sold quickly. There are a lot of Amish around here, so I'm hoping it will happen fast."

She shrugged, even though she knew Melissa couldn't see her. "We'll see how it goes. Say a prayer for me."

"I'll get the whole office praying for you," Melissa replied. "Let me know if you need anything."

"Just those prayers."

The women hung up and Helena wandered through the house, looking for the internet password as the skies grew darker, the rain pattering faster and harder over the house as the hours passed.

Eventually, Helena found the information she needed for the internet, tucked away in a drawer with lightbulbs and random chargers.

Relieved, she plugged her laptop into one of the outlets and began to work, the rhythm of the storm playing a song to her in the background as the grayish light of the squall melted away to a darkness outside the wide, rectangular windows in the kitchen.

Helena broke from her work once to find coffee, rubbing her sooty eyes and checking the time, her stomach growling, but she ignored it and filled herself with coffee, as usual, before returning to work. She would eat when she had finished working.

The rain grew louder, the thunder and lightning directly overhead, some of it so close, it made the house shake and the lights flicker.

Suddenly, there was a loud crash from outside, freezing Helena in her chair. Her head swiveled toward the kitchen window, another flash of white streaking against the night sky. A yelp of terror escaped her mouth as the outline of a human figure appeared at the window.

Helena leapt up from her spot, her heart hammering as she rushed toward the knife block, grabbing for the first blade she could find, but when she looked toward the window again, she saw nothing.

My eyes are tired from staring at the computer screen too long, she tried to convince herself but her pulse wouldn't slow down, her heart directly in her throat as she ambled slowly toward the back door, eyes blinking rapidly as she closed her hand tightly around the wooden handle of the knife.

"H-hello?" she yelled out, refusing to let the matter go. "Who's there?"

I've seen this horror movie, she scolded herself, slowly opening the heavy door, praying vigorously to God as she pried it open. *Don't be a fool! Call the police!*

But she did none of those things as she stepped into the rain, the blackness encompassing her.

"Hello! Is someone out here?" she mewled again, refusing to let the matter go. A small cry met her ears over the storm and her arm fell to her side, her gaze landing on a crumbled, shivering form near the back step. For a long moment, Helena merely gaped at it, sure she was seeing things, but when he lifted his head, she realized that her eyes were not playing tricks.

"Oh, my goodness!" she gasped, setting the knife down and rushing toward the trembling, sobbing figure. This was no horror movie figure. It was a little boy of five years or so, soaked to the core and terrified.

CHAPTER 2

*H*elena stared into the wide, scared blue eyes of the boy, her immediate thought that an angel had been dropped on her back doorstep. He was so small, drenched and clearly petrified. But all the way out here and by himself? None of this made sense to her.

"Who are you?" she blurted out. "What are you doing here?"

He cowered at her tone and she advanced on him more, shaking her head in the driving rain. For a moment, she merely gaped at him, unsure of what to say or do with him.

He's just a kid, Lena! Get him inside! a voice cried out in her head. It snapped her to her senses.

"Come inside, please! You're going to get sick out here like this."

She had no way of knowing how long he had already been out there, but judging by the way he was soaked all the way through, she guessed it had been a while. "Please," she said again, lowering her voice. "I'm Helena. What's your name?"

He lifted his head and gaped at her, shivering violently as Helena extended a hand. "C-Caleb."

"Caleb, it's warm inside and I have some soup. Do you like chicken noodle?" she pressed. "It will warm you right up. Please. Come in where it's safe."

He bit down on his lower lip as she shifted her weight, stepping back under the overhang to study his homespun clothes.

He's Amish. What the heck is he doing all the way out here by himself?

"Caleb, I don't want to stand in the rain," she said sternly. "I'm going inside, and I want you to come with me."

She turned away but left the door open for him to follow, hoping that he would. To her utter relief, he padded in behind her, his boots making a slopping sound with every step. Helena retreated to the pantry and found one of the cans of chicken noodle soup she had seen earlier, setting a pot onto the gas stove as Caleb entered and closed the door. She steeled her breaths before talking again, reminding herself that he was the one in trouble, not her.

"How old are you?" she asked, gauging his age again.

"F-five, nearly six." His teeth were chattering. She disappeared onto the second floor, locating some fresh towels and returned to hand them to the boy.

He took them and haphazardly dried himself. She wanted to help him, but she didn't dare, not knowing him or understanding what was going on. Instead, she settled for cooking the soup as she studied him suspiciously. "Where are your family, Caleb?"

To her dismay, tears flooded his eyes. "I don't know!" he whined, throwing the towels aside and folding his arms defiantly over his chest.

"What do you mean you don't know? Did you lose them in the storm, get separated from them?"

That would explain why he's so scared.

She turned off the stove and carefully poured the soup into a bowl, sliding it across the wooden island toward him.

The boy shook his mop of tangled black hair, avoiding her eyes, but he didn't answer, his mouth already full of soup. Impatiently, Helena waited for him to eat, holding off on any more questions until he had finished devouring what was in his bowl.

She was reluctant to offer him anymore, unsure if she was feeding the child something he wasn't allowed to be eating out of a can.

In the end, she decided it didn't matter since he had already consumed the first bowl. "Do want some more?"

His wide, round, blue eyes widened, but he shook his head vehemently, his cheeks reddening. She waited for him to say something else, but when he didn't speak, she offered her own thoughts.

"I don't have any clothes that will fit you," she told him. "But maybe I can drive you home. Do you know where you live?"

His bottom lip jutted out and Helena smothered another sigh, sensing the defiance all over him. "*Nee.*"

Her eyes narrowed into slits, reading the blatant lie covering his innocent face.

Why doesn't he want to go home? What is he doing out here at this time of night, by himself, in the middle of a storm?

A dozen terrible thoughts rushed through Helena's mind, but she kept them to herself, careful not to lead the answer out of him.

"Honey, you can't stay here. Your family must be worried sick about you. Your mother will be out of her mind."

"My *mudder* is dead," the child said flatly. Panic overcame her as she considered the implications of what he was saying.

"When did that happen? Now? Tonight?" she demanded, straightening. Suddenly, his presence made sense if he were running around, looking for help.

Oh my God! And I've been sitting here, feeding him soup!

"*Nee!*" Caleb grumbled impatiently. "A long time ago. She went to the *Englisch* hospital and never came *deheem*."

Helena's heart cracked as she made sense of his English littered sentence and his small face turned away.

"Oh…" Helena swallowed thickly, the memory of her own lost parents springing to mind sharply and unexpectedly. "I-I'm sorry to hear that, Caleb. Who do you live with then if your mother is gone?"

His head jerked up. "My *bruder* and *vadder*," he announced almost angrily. "But Danny is gone, too!"

Helena leaned across the counter and peered into his impassioned face. "Is Danny your brother?" she asked kindly. Caleb nodded, shivering, and she backed away to find him a throw blanket from the back of the sofa. Gratefully, the boy wrapped himself up in the warm fabric and stared at her.

"What do you mean he's gone?" she asked gently. "Is he…?"

She couldn't bring herself to ask him the horrible question, but to her relief, Caleb spared her from finishing her own sentence.

"He left for the *schtadt* two days ago and he hasn't *komme deheem*." Tears blurred at Caleb's eyes as Helena gawked at him.

"I-I'm sorry, Caleb. I don't know what any of that means," she said slowly, trying to make sense of the little boy's distress. "You need to speak to me in English. I don't speak…your language."

He refused to look at her, his eyes fixed on the countertop, but Helena had enough of this back and forth. She could not keep the child here when she was sure people were out looking for him.

"Caleb, I'm going to get my purse and keys and we're going for a ride in my car," she told him sternly. "I need to find your house. Do you think if we go for a little ride, you might be able to tell me which house is yours?"

He shook his head defiantly and Helena's brow creased.

"Why not?"

"We have to go to the city to find my *bruder*—my brother, Daniel," Caleb cried out passionately. "He's gone away."

Helena paused. "Why has he gone away?" she asked slowly. Her head beginning to throb.

"*Daed* says for *Rumspringa*," Caleb moaned, a tear dropping down his cheeks. "But he's been gone for days!"

Sympathy for the boy overtook her, but her sense of concern for the child's family far bypassed her pity. "Caleb, if you don't come with me, I'll have to call the police to come and get you," she informed him, gently but firmly. "I don't want to get Children's Service's involved, but you're not leaving me much of a choice if you don't go home."

Terror struck the child's face and Helena saw that she had spoken the proper words.

"Come on," she urged him, reaching for her purse off the counter. "Let's get you home."

She turned toward the front door as Caleb slipped off the stool, but before they could make it to the front door, a loud banging caused Helena to choke and jump in shock.

"*Pliese!*" Caleb begged, cowering back behind the wall between the kitchen and foyer. "I don't want to go with anyone but you."

"Caleb—"

"I'm not going with anyone! I'll run off again!"

Frowning, Helena strode toward the door and threw it open. A worried older man stood dripping on her front stoop. His straw hat sat askew on his salt and pepper head, his full beard littered with diamond water droplets. He was clearly Amish, and his dark eyes were shadowed with deep concern.

This is the strangest night of my life.

"I'm very sorry to disturb you, Madam," he said, his deep voice laced with a hint of an accent. "I'm looking for a young boy from our community."

"Are you his father?" Helena asked, glancing over her shoulder toward Caleb, who had disappeared from view. She gritted her teeth together, hoping that the child didn't sneak out the back door, but she suspected he might if she turned him in.

The man's eyes widened. "Have you seen him?"

"Are you his father?" she asked again, refusing to respond as she crossed her arms over her chest.

"No…" He appeared annoyed by her pointed question. "I am one of the ministers and a neighbor of the family. The boy's father is very concerned about him."

"Caleb *is* here," Helena informed him, watching the man's face relax, a smidgen of guilt sliding through her. "But I won't release him to anyone but his father."

The minister didn't like Helena's answer, and she did not much blame him.

"He can come with me—"

"I don't know you," Helena insisted firmly. "And I'm not letting a five-year-old go with a stranger."

He stiffened. "With respect, Madam, *you are* a stranger here."

"And yet Caleb chose to come to *my* house," Helena retorted. "Bring the boy's father here and he can take Caleb home. He'll be here waiting."

The minister hesitated, attempting to peer over Helena's shoulder, but she blocked his view.

"Is he all right?" he asked and Helena softened.

"Yes. He's fine. He's eaten and is warm and dry now," she reassured the older man. With a deep exhale, the stranger backed away from the porch and headed toward his restless horse in the driving rain beyond.

"Joseph Lantz will be here shortly. Please have Caleb ready," the minister instructed, climbing onto the bench and disappearing into the night. Helena closed the front door and turned toward the child who had come out of his hiding spot.

"You're causing a lot of trouble in your community, Caleb," she scolded him. "That poor man is soaked and very worried about you."

Caleb hung his head, saying nothing.

"You will go home with your father when he arrives," Helena added. "I don't want any fight about it."

Caleb visibly swallowed and nodded, but his misery was almost palpable. Her voice softened as she knelt in front of him. "I'm sure your brother will be home soon, too," she said. "But you can't run off again looking for him, all right?"

The boy still didn't speak, and Helena wondered if she was getting through to him at all.

Rising, she stifled a sigh and extended her hand toward him. "Come on," she said, nodding toward the living room. "Let's go watch some television while we're waiting, okay?"

Caleb's eyes popped. "Television?" he echoed and Helena winced, recognizing her faux pas too late.

The Amish don't watch tv. What the heck do Amish kids do?

"Er...or maybe we'll read a book instead," she suggested quickly. She hoped this Joseph would hurry up and come soon. Helen didn't know the first thing about tending to children—especially not Amish children with whom she had nothing in common.

CHAPTER 3

*R*ain dribbled down Joseph Lantz's shirt collar, bathing his skin in water, but he barely noticed as he pulled his buggy back toward his house. Lights still flickered in the window sills but there was no sign of his young son, tears blurring his vision as he dismounted his wagon, ignoring his disgruntled horse who snorted and stomped, clearly hoping to be sheltered from the storm after hours of being out in search of young Caleb.

Why didn't I pay him more mind? Joseph asked himself, spinning around in the darkness, considering more places to check for the boy. He felt as though he had searched every nook and cranny of the district in the darkness, every hiding spot that Caleb may have found himself in the night, to no avail at all. He wished that Daniel was there to help him search. Surely his older brother would know of better hiding places.

Of course, Caleb would not be hiding if Daniel were there.

The neighbors had been searching with him for hours, combing their houses and barns in case Caleb had snuck inside to hide among the horses or chickens, but so far there had been no word on the child and as the hours passed, Joseph was beginning to lose hope of ever finding the little boy.

His heart pounded with terror and fear, his mind whirling as he considered what might have become of Caleb.

Would he have gotten in a car with an Englischer passing by? Would they have taken him to Broken Wheel?

Joseph had notified the Bishop about Caleb's disappearance, and he was sure that the elder would have gone to speak with the police in town, just in case the child ended up there, but the idea flooded Joseph with dread. He would have some serious explaining to do if that were the case. The English already looked down upon the way the Amish managed their children and a case with the government might be opened if Caleb had made it that far. Children's Services might pay them a visit and he had heard dreadful stories of families losing their children for less.

I can't lose Caleb, too.

Joseph entered his house, dripping water all over the front of his entranceway, his hat falling off in his hands. He barely made it into the living room when he dropped to his knees, bowing his head in prayer.

Pliese, Gott, wherever Caleb is, just let him be safe. I will deal with the aftermath of it all. Just bring my bu deheem to me.

He was consumed with regret and shame, the memory of how withdrawn Caleb had become when his brother Daniel had left for Rumspringa, but Joseph had been far too busy with his farm to pay the child much mind. Rumspringa was a rite of passage, after all. Every young Amish person experienced it, and Daniel was no different. He had been so sure that Caleb would get over his sulking and move on. It never occurred to Joseph that Caleb might go after his brother—not that he had been paying much mind in the springtime planting. There was simply too much to do with Daniel gone and the widower being on his own.

Bring him deheem safe, he prayed to God, rocking on his haunches in front of the unlit hearth as the storm continued to rage on outside. He wished his older son were there to give him sensible words of comfort or advice, to reassure him that despite his youth, Caleb was savvy and smart enough to know his way around the district and would not get in a vehicle with someone he did not know.

Yet if that were true, how had no one seen him? Surely someone in the community would have caught sight of the boy after all these hours already.

What if he's hurt and no one can hear him? What if he's lost...?

Lost in his prayers, Joseph did not hear the buggy approach his house over the driving rain, nor the footsteps on his porch until someone pounded frantically on the door.

"Joe! Joey!"

Blinking, Joesph was on his feet, rushing toward the foyer to throw open the front door, his heart hammering in a panic as one of the ministers stood drenched on the patio.

"Eli! *Wat* is it? Do you have news?" he gasped, afraid of what his neighbor's response might be.

"I've found him!" Eli Troyer announced, and a deep sense of relief almost brought Joseph to his knees again as he rushed outside, but the minister held up his hands to stop him. "He's not here."

Confused, Joseph froze, peering at the older man. "Why not? Is he hurt? Oh no, *wat* has happened?"

Eli shook his head, placing a reassuring hand on his friend's shoulder. "He's not hurt, and he's not far away," Eli said quickly. "But the *frau* won't release him to anyone but you."

There was a hint of bitterness in his tone as Joseph continued to gape at him uncomprehendingly. "*Wat frau? Wat* are you saying?"

"Caleb is at the Berry *haus*," Eli explained quickly. "Just up the road."

Joseph's brow creased into a vee of perplexity. "But Clyde is dead," he said bluntly. "The *haus* is empty."

"*Nee*," Eli explained. "There is a *frau* there now...a relative, I assume. Caleb is at the *haus* with her."

Joseph had heard enough and closed the door behind him, rushing back toward his buggy as Eli followed. "Why didn't you bring him home?" Joseph grumbled, but a clap of thunder blocked Eli's response as he climbed onto the bench of his buggy, and he was off down the muddy road without looking to see if his neighbor was following.

A fusion of gratefulness and deeper concern twined in his heart as he urged his protesting horse along through the mud, the wheels sticking every so often along the country roads, but Joseph refused to stop. He would not rest until he laid eyes on his son.

He must have gone to the Berry haus thinking it was empty. Why didn't I check there?

It had not occurred to him, but he was glad that Eli had considered it.

With his hammering heart, he urged the horse to move faster, ignoring the pelting rain over his face as the well-lit house came into view from the black road. A silver vehicle sat near the front door, the porch light brightly illuminating the way as Joseph dismounted and rushed forward, stumbling across the uneven ground.

Ich bin oom cooma, Caleb, he told his son silently, his panic finally diminishing. He vowed he would pay better attention to Caleb's despair going forward.

CHAPTER 4

"*I* think your dad is here," Helena commented, dropping the curtain to rise from the sofa as the weary figure shuffled toward the front door.

Caleb sat sullenly on the couch, his arms folded as she moved toward the door to allow the man entry.

"You remember our deal, Caleb? You have to go with him now."

The boy still said nothing.

As the door opened, Helena found herself startled, his vivid blue eyes almost identical to that of the boy's who sat in the room at her back. His black hair was plastered to his angular face, the concern etched almost to the bone.

There's no doubt whose kid that boy is, Helena mused ruefully, her pulse pounding unexpectedly. She would not require identification in any form.

"Are you Joseph?" she asked before he could utter a word. He cleared his throat and looked down as if he realized he, too, was holding her gaze.

"*Yah*—yes," he mumbled. "Is my son here?"

"Yes," she replied, stepping back to let him inside. "Come on in. Get out of the rain."

Reluctantly, he stepped over the threshold, his bright blue eyes darting over the entranceway until they landed on his child. "Caleb!"

Slowly, the boy rose from his chair, his small head hung in shame, but Joseph didn't appear angry in the least. He strode across the foyer, oblivious and uncaring of the water he dripped along the way as he embraced his son, the relief oozing from his tall frame. "I was so worried!" he choked. "Oh, *denki* goodness, you're all right."

Helena stood back, unbothered by the mess Joseph had made, particularly when Caleb began to relax in his father's arms.

"You're not mad?" the little one whispered. Joseph shook his head, clinging to his son as he tipped his head back toward the roof, his lips moving silently. Helena realized he was praying and her heart warmed at the sight.

"I'm not mad," Joesph managed to say, finally releasing him. "*Komme.* Let's get you *deheem.* You've taken up enough of this *frau's* time."

He turned to her gratefully. "*Denki*—er, thank you. Thank you for keeping my son safe."

"No!" Helena cried out before she could stop herself. Both sets of eyes fell on her and she flushed, offering them a grin.

"I mean, the weather is still awful and Caleb is safe now. Why don't I put on some coffee and you can wait it out a while? Hopefully it will let up in a bit and then you can head out."

Joseph hesitated, but Caleb nodded vehemently. *"Yah, Daed. Can we stay a little longer? Helena is nett."*

Warily, Joesph eyed her and Helena shrugged nonchalantly. "I really don't mind. It would make me feel better than sending you back out there in this storm, honestly. Caleb only just got dry, really. It would be a shame to get him all soaked again."

She flashed Joseph a winning smile, and he relented. "Maybe for a few minutes," he agreed begrudgingly. His eyes bugged as he looked down to see himself making a mess of the floor and Joseph immediately backed up toward the door, mumbling apologetically.

"It's all right," Helena reassured him with a small laugh. "It's only water. Come inside. I'll put a pot of coffee on. Caleb, why don't you show him the way?"

Proudly, the boy puffed out his chest as Helena headed into the back of the house, casting the handsome father another sneaking glance. She had not expected to see such an attractive widower on her doorstep, but she reminded herself she really did not have time for this.

I'm just being hospitable. The man was worried about his kid. I'm being a decent human being.

Or at least that's what she told herself as she busied her hands in the huge farmhouse kitchen.

"Wat were you thinking, running off like that?" she heard Joseph chiding his son gently as the pair joined her in the room. "Everyone has been looking for you, for hours!"

"I went to find Danny!" Caleb insisted defiantly, not a hint of remorse in his tone.

"Cale, Danny has gone to the city for Rumspringa. He'll be *deheem* soon."

"You said that about *Mamm* too!" Caleb retorted sharply. Joseph fell silent, sinking into one of the kitchen chairs tiredly. Helena tried not to listen, but it was difficult when she stood so close.

"Caleb, your *mudder* was very *grank*. Danny is not sick." The handsome father cast Helena an apologetic look. "I am sorry for all this. He is missing his brother, who has gone away for a little while."

Helena leaned back on the counter, nodding. "I know. Caleb explained it a bit to me and I did tell him the same thing— that his brother would be home soon."

Joseph's eyes widened appreciatively. "Oh? Do you know about *Amisch* traditions?"

She chuckled before she could stop herself and immediately dropped her chin in embarrassment. "No. I'm sorry. I don't know much about your customs, but I think I've heard about Rumspringa. That's where your young people go and live in the city for a while to experience the outside world, right? I've seen the kids in Akron from time to time."

Joseph nodded slowly. "Yes…it's very important that they experience the world beyond our community before they decide if they want to be baptized or not."

Helena was stunned by the revelation. "They aren't baptized at birth?"

Joseph shook his head. "No…we believe in allowing everyone to make the choice when they are old enough. Adults should find *Gott* on their own terms."

Impressed, Helena turned toward the percolating coffee maker. "I had no idea," she said honestly.

"Danny might stay in the city," Caleb whimpered.

"That very rarely happens, Cale," Joseph told his son. "Do you know of any *kinner* who have stayed in the city after *Rumspringa*?"

Helena's curiosity was fully piqued now, the sincerity in Joseph's tone startling.

Really? They all come back?

She couldn't imagine living like they did, without all the creature comforts she enjoyed so much, but she believed every word Joseph spoke. He had such a gentle, pure way about him.

Listening for Caleb's response, she poured coffee into two chipped mugs she had found in the cupboard over the stove and padded toward the table to sit with Joseph and the boy.

Caleb had no answer, his eyes fixed on the table.

"Danny will be back, *sohn*," Joseph went on. "But I am sorry I didn't listen to you more closely when you spoke about your concerns. I promise I will now."

Helena offered the child a warm smile. "You see, Caleb? You have nothing to worry about. Your brother will come home, just like everyone else does."

Her gaze traveled up toward his father and their eyes inadvertently locked, causing a flash of heat to touch

Helena's cheeks. Hastily, she picked up her mug and took a long sip, clearing her throat as she set her eyes anywhere but on Joseph's face.

"You're Clyde's daughter?" Joseph asked unexpectedly. Helena's head jerked back toward him.

"No." She chuckled nervously. "I'm his niece. He was my father's brother."

"Ah, *yah*. I didn't think he had any *kinner* of his own," Joseph said, nodding.

"Did you know my uncle?"

"A little bit. He was a *gut mann*. Quiet. Respectful. We did business sometimes."

She suddenly realized she hadn't properly introduced herself. "I'm Helena. Berry. Same as Clyde."

Dear God. I'm babbling.

She clamped her mouth closed and put the mug back to her lips again to stop herself from saying anything else foolish.

"Joseph Lantz," he introduced himself.

"Good to meet you, Joseph." Another quick smiled touched the edges of Helena's mouth but she looked away, feeling the tips of her diamond-studded earlobes get hot.

"Your *onkle* was hard to know," Joseph told her. "He kept to himself, mostly."

"That sounds like Uncle Clyde," Helena agreed. "Honestly, I didn't know him at all. Inheriting this place was a bit of a shock to me."

Joseph sat back in his chair to study her face pensively. "Have you given any thought as to what you'll do with it?"

Helena blinked once. "With the house?"

"The house, the cattle, the land," he replied, sitting forward to set his forearms on the table. "Our land is right next door—although it doesn't seem that way with the fields in between."

Helena's eyebrows knit. "Okay…?"

"If you are looking to sell the property, I would be interested in buying it."

Caleb made a sound, and the adults peered at him. A scowl formed on his face.

"Sit straight, Cale," his father instructed him. Obediently, he did what he was asked, and they returned to their conversation, excitement sparking in Helena's gut.

"Really?" she asked slowly. "All of it?"

"I don't know," Joseph answered truthfully. "I know I am most interested in the land, and probably the cattle too, but I have never had occasion to look at Clyde's stock. I won't have any use for the house…probably. Daniel might want it for when he gets married, but that's a discussion I would have to have with him when he returns."

Helena's head began to spin, the conversation moving much faster than she had expected.

"I only arrived here today," she confessed. "I hired a realtor to put the house on the market, but I can call him in the morning if you want to do a private sale…"

She trailed off uncertainly. "I don't know enough about farm inventory to do this on my own," she admitted.

Joseph nodded. "I understand. You don't know me, but I can promise you a fair price and I'll give you time to check with others in the area to compare my offer."

I trust you, she almost blurted out, but stopped herself, gnawing on the insides of her cheeks before the words could slip out.

"I don't have any use for this property, or the livestock," she conceded slowly. "The sooner I can get this matter resolved, the sooner I can get back to my life in Akron."

Joseph stood, gesturing for Caleb to do the same, but Helena could not help but notice the slightly baleful look that the boy gave her.

"Let me go home and put together an offer for you as you go through the contents of the property," Joseph suggested. "We can meet again tomorrow—and hopefully the storm will have cleared by then."

Caleb grunted rudely, and his father chided him. "Caleb!"

"*Wat's* so special about the city?" he grouched, trudging after Joseph as the older man led the way to the front door. "Why does everyone want to go there?"

Helena's lips parted to tout the virtues of her life in Akron, but she stopped herself. She couldn't explain any of it to a boy who had lived so simply his whole life, nor did she want to ruin his idyllic life with a father who obviously loved him very much.

"I don't know," she fibbed instead. "It is very beautiful out here. I would stay if I could."

"Then you should stay, too," Caleb suggested. Helena stifled a snort, but as she opened the door to let the Lantzes out into the drizzling night, Joesph's stare again locked on hers. Another shiver of pleasure rushed through her.

I can see some of the merits of living out here, she conceded silently, bidding them goodnight. But this was no life for a woman like Helena Berry.

CHAPTER 5

*J*oesph was unsure what to do about Caleb after they returned home. A part of him wanted to scold him for putting not only him but the entire district through so much trouble, particularly during a storm, but he knew he could not fault his young son for acting like a boy of his age. He had already lost his mother and the fear of losing his brother had made him behave irrationally.

"Are you mad, *Daed?*" Caleb asked meekly from his spot by the living room window as he watched the storm passing. A light rain continued to pour outside, but the thunder had subsided, and the lightning had passed far down the fields, almost entirely out of view. In an hour, it would all be gone, a distant memory, like Caleb's disappearance.

Joseph was barely able to answer him when the back door opened and Eli Troyer appeared with his wife, tracking mud with them through the kitchen in their hurriedness.

"Oh, *denki* goodness!" Leah Troyer gasped, setting her sights on Caleb. "He's all right!"

"*Yah*, he's fine," Joseph agreed, swallowing a cringe to see the mess on his floors. He did not have the time to clean as often as he would like and now he would have to take time to deal with this new problem in the morning before he began the day's chores.

"How *deerich*!" Eli scolded the boy, who blanched and cowered as the minister advanced on him. "Do you have any idea how much trouble you caused everyone!"

"That's enough, Eli," Joseph said sternly, stepping between his son and the elder, shaking his head. "Caleb knows what he did was wrong."

"He ought to be punished for it!" Eli insisted. Joseph's brow furrowed in annoyance.

"This is a *familye* matter, Eli," he said quietly.

The older man made a reproving sound. "It wasn't so much a *familye* matter when you needed *hilf* looking for the *bu*, was it?"

Caleb released a whimper of fear, but Leah interjected. "*Komme*, Eli. It's been a long *nacht*. Let's leave them to get settled, *yah*?"

"If you go too easy on him, he'll just do it again—and worse!" the minister warned. "And then you won't have anyone to *hilf* you because he'll be the *bu* who cried wolf, *yah*?"

Joseph wriggled his lips to keep from responding, catching his son's panicked expression as Leah Troyer ushered her husband out of the house.

"*Es dutt mer leed, Daed*," Caleb moaned, tears filling his eyes the moment the back door closed, and they were left on their own. "I-I only wanted to find Danny!"

"I know why you did it, Caleb, but it doesn't make it right," Joseph replied sternly. "You could have been hurt or someone else could have been hurt looking for you in that *schtarm*. Would you be able to forgive yourself if you were responsible for someone else's injury?"

Shame flooded the child's eyes, and Joseph's heart seized.

I went too far with that, he thought, missing his wife terribly in that moment. Miriam was much better with discipline than he had ever been.

"I won't do it again!" Caleb implored him. "I promise!"

Joseph believed him. He drew closer to the boy, kneeling in front of him and taking his hands.

"You should pray to *Gott* for forgiveness for this, not me," he instructed, and Caleb nodded quickly, bowing his head. For several minutes, father and son were silent, each lost in their private conversations with God. But Joseph found his own thoughts straying from Caleb and more toward Clyde Berry's attractive niece, who had shocked him upon his arrival.

He had not expected anyone to be at the house, least of all someone as pretty and sensible as Helena, but he knew he could not allow himself to consider her like that.

Lifting his head, he cleared his throat quietly and Caleb's small chin jutted upward, his vivid blue eyes imploring as he searched for signs of dismay on his father's face.

"You should get ready for bed," Joseph instructed him. "It's getting late."

Caleb rose from his knees, but he did not move as his father did the same. "*Daed?*"

"*Wat* is it, Cale?"

"Do you miss *Mamm?*"

The query took Joseph aback, his chest constricting at the mere mention of his late wife after so long. Miriam's name did not often arise in the house, particularly not from Caleb's lips.

For a half a moment, Joseph considered dismissing his son, sending him to bed and ignoring the painful discussion, but immediately he was overcome with shame by the thought.

Discounting his feelings is what led to all this trouble tonight in the first place, he reminded himself.

"*Hoch dich anne,*" he told Caleb, gesturing for the boy to sit. Obligingly, Caleb climbed onto the sofa and Joseph took the wing chair across from the lowly lit fireplace where the pair had been warming themselves by the flames. "*Yah*, Cale. I do miss your *mudder,* very much. I think about her every day, but she is with *Gott* now. You know that."

Caleb bobbed his head quickly, lowering his gaze. "*Yah*, I know that," he agreed. "But I wanted to know if you get lonely."

The man's eyebrows shot up in surprise. It was a very astute question for such a young boy. "I have a lot to keep myself *bissi,*" he answered evasively. "The farm and you boys…"

"But it's hard without *Mamm*," Caleb insisted. "You have to cook and clean, too."

"*Yah*, Caleb, it is hard without a *weib*," he conceded, wondering where his youngest son was going with such pointed questions. He soon had his answer, however.

"Would you ever get married again?"

Pursing his lips, Joseph eyed the child. "*Yah*, it's a possibility, Caleb. Why are you asking this?"

"Helena is nice."

Understanding washed through Joseph in a torrent, and he sucked in a sharp breath. "Ah."

"You don't think she's nice?" Caleb questioned defensively.

"She seems very nice," Joseph said with a sigh. "But Caleb, she isn't *Amisch*."

His declaration was met with a blank stare, as if the boy could not understand why he was stating such a fact.

I should have waited for another day to have this conversation.

"I couldn't marry Helena, even if she were interested—which I don't believe she would be. Her intentions are to sell her *onkle's haus* and return to her life in the city."

Caleb paled. "You don't know that! You didn't ask her!"

"You were there when she said as much."

"But that was before she met us!" Caleb insisted. "She could change her mind!"

Joseph stifled the urge to argue with the child. Caleb was far too young to understand the intimacies of adult relationships, particularly when it pertained to the English.

"It's late, Cale. You should get some rest, *yah*?"

"But you should speak to Helena!" he insisted. "Will you speak to her? Maybe she wants to get married too!"

Joseph did not want to give his son false hope, but he could also see that Caleb would not easily leave the matter alone.

"I will see her in the *mariye*," he reminded Caleb. "I will talk to her about her plans."

Relief fell over Caleb's face, but it only filled Joseph with shame. It was clear that Helena had been kind to Caleb, but that did not change the fact that she was not one of them. The sooner she left Broken Wheel and returned to Akron, the better off everyone would be.

Ensuring that Caleb was tucked into bed, Joseph wandered through the huge house, turning off the lanterns and putting out the fire in the hearth before retiring to his own room. He lingered by Daniel's bedroom door, half expecting his older son to be in bed, as always. A pang of loneliness shot over him as Caleb's words echoed through his mind.

Daniel is almost of marrying age and then Caleb will be too. I should think about marrying again.

Of course, he could not entertain the idea of courting Helena Berry, not seriously, even if she were to remain in Broken Wheel. Why, then, could he not get the idea out of his mind?

Much as he tried to cast the notion aside, the image of her lovely gray eyes filtered behind his own closed lids when he tucked himself into bed and drifted off to sleep.

Sleep came easily for Joseph that night, the pitter-patter of raindrops lulling him into an exhausted slumber, the emotional toll of the day catching up with him. But his dream was unlike any he had ever had before.

He recalled every part of it as if he were reading it in a book, the sky above his head clear and cloudless, the blue surreal sun shining endlessly.

Helena stood next to Clyde's house in a proper, homespun dress, her prayer bonnet capturing every strand of her red hair.

It's the wrong color. She's married. To whom?

But the dream spelled out quite simply who Helena belonged to, the pair smiling affectionately at one another, even from the distance between them.

He stood on the porch, watching her paint the picket fence surrounding the property as Caleb ran through the connecting fields, exclaiming excitedly about a baby.

"It's going to be a *bu*! I want a *bruder*! I want a *bruder*!" Caleb cheered.

"You have a *bruder*," Joseph said and laughed as Daniel appeared from around the side of the house, a young lady on his arm, although her face was obstructed by the blinding rays of the sun.

"I'm your *bruder*," Daniel reminded him.

"The *bobbli* will be whatever the *bobbli* is," Helena said sweetly, without missing a single brushstroke. "*Bu* or *maedel*, we will love the *bobbli* just the same."

The dream felt so real that when Joseph woke, he immediately reached out for Helena and found himself embarrassed as dawn fully woke him.

It felt more like a vision than a dream.

Don't be narricht, he scolded himself, hastily rising to feed his son before starting his day. He grimaced to see the filth on the kitchen floor from all the mud that had been tracked in the previous night by Eli and Leah Yoder. Joseph had forgotten about the cleaning that would need to be done before his usual day began. Sighing, he located the broom and then the mop and began his cleaning, determined not to complain.

Maybe these are all signs from Gott, he mused, feeling slightly foolish about the thoughts. Helena Berry had a full English life in the city. For all he knew, she had a boyfriend or a prospective husband already.

But he would not know unless he asked, he reasoned, and he had promised to visit that day with a proper number for a potential purchase. If she rejected him, he would know for sure and be able to tell Caleb that he had tried.

And if she doesn't?

His heartbeat quickened at the unbidden idea.

Maybe that dream truly did mean something.

"Guten mariye, Daed."

His son's voice shattered his mental dilemma and Joseph smiled quickly, setting the mop aside as Caleb sat at the scarred kitchen table.

"Guten mariye," he greeted Caleb with a smile.

"Are we going to see Helena *heit?*" the boy asked without preamble.

I'm not the only one with her on my mind, it seems.

Caleb stared imploringly at his father and Joseph decided, setting aside his nervousness. "*Yah*, we are," he said before he could change his mind.

I will hope for the best but expect the worst. But no matter what, I will accept her choice.

CHAPTER 6

*I*n truth, it didn't really surprise her, but Helena could not sleep a wink at her uncle's house. She chalked it up to the drafty, old structure, and then the storm. The lumpy old mattress didn't help matters, and she dreamt of her own comfortable memory foam bed, waiting for her in Akron.

The unfamiliarity of the countryside kept her pacing the long hallways and taking notes on all the furnishings and belongings until a pale gray light filtered through the daybreak, well before six a.m.

It was only as she started making coffee and peered out the back door to see the day laborers approaching that she realized she had been thinking about Joseph Lantz and his young son for half the night, at least. The discomfort had little to do with her surroundings and mostly to do with what was happening in her own mind.

They'll be over soon with an amount. I should let the laborers know that their days are numbered here—or at least that there's going to be new ownership. It's the right thing to do.

With a mug of steaming coffee in her hand, she slipped her heels on and padded out into the soft grass to greet the workers, who began herding the cows into the lush pastures beyond. Her shoes sunk into the ground, still soft from the storm.

But Helena barely noticed, her eyes taking in the loveliness of the Ohio landscape, the sun breaking brilliantly over the horizon as she found the nearest worker.

"Good morning," she said brightly. The young man eyed her inappropriate outfit, the oversized and hole-ridden robe she had found in her uncle's closet wrapped around her, her pumps poking out beneath the frayed plaid fabric.

"Good morning," he conceded tersely. "You're coming to fire us, aren't you?"

"Oh." Helena laughed nervously. "That's not why I'm here. I'm glad you're still here. I didn't even realize there were cows until after you guys had left yesterday. I really don't know what's going to happen coming up, honestly. I'm selling the property and the new owners might keep you on."

He raised an eyebrow with thinly veiled disdain.

I'm definitely not meant to be a farmer.

"Okay. Then what do you want?"

Helena swallowed, forgetting the whole speech she had prepared.

"I'm wondering if you know how much a cow sells for," she added quickly, sensing that he didn't want to chitchat.

He snorted. "That depends on the breed, the age and the sex —it's not a number you just pull out of the sky."

"Right." Helena sighed, again feeling as if she was in over her head. "And who would I talk to about all that?"

The young man shrugged indifferently. "Your uncle should have records on all the animals. There would be a price attached in the records."

He shuffled off before Helena could question him more and her heart sank as she stood back, wishing that all of this had not fallen on her shoulders.

Simultaneously, she could not help but wonder how Clyde had managed to keep the farm on his own.

Maybe he has a bookkeeper I don't know about?

As the sun rose fully, she was consumed by the beauty of the property, an ache of melancholy touching her for an instant.

Would he want me to keep it? Is that why he gave it to me?

She exhaled, shaking off the thought as she retreated to the house, her feet sinking deeper into the mud, the shoes completely ruined by the time she reached the back door. One of the rubber caps on the back of her heels had fallen off in the walk and she grunted.

Inside, she headed upstairs to dress in the only tracksuit she'd brought, and as she returned to the main floor, her ears caught the faintest clip-clopping of horse hooves outside.

A burst of excitement rushed through her as she immediately suspected who had come to visit, her hand on the doorknob as a sharp rap echoed through the foyer. She'd barely opened the front door when Caleb came barreling through.

"Caleb, mind your manners," his father scolded him, but Helena didn't mind, his small arms embracing her at the waist. A little laugh fell from her lips, her own arms encircling his shoulders.

"Good morning!" she said happily, pleased to see the boy's face shining and alert. He almost seemed like a different boy compared to the child she had found huddled by the back steps in the pouring rain the evening before.

"*Guten mariye*," Caleb replied, enunciating each word deliberately and clearly. He stared pointedly at Helena and she realized he expected her to repeat them.

"*Guten mariye*," she offered, the words rolling off her tongue easily.

Joseph's brow shot up, his expression impressed. "You speak *Deutsch*?" he gasped in shock.

"Goodness, no!" Helena chuckled, ushering the father and son inside the house and securing the door in their wake. "But I did take a few German classes in high school. It's not that much different, is it?"

"Our language has Germanic roots," Joseph conceded. "You have a very *gut* accent."

Helen found herself inordinately pleased with the compliment and beamed broadly at her guest. "Come, I have a fresh pot of coffee on. Are you hungry, Caleb?"

"*Nee, nee*," Joseph interjected. "He's just had breakfast."

"The men are outside with the cows right now," Helena explained. "I was trying to get an idea on what it will cost to sell them but I don't think they're very happy with me because I can't give them any definitive answers about work."

She sank down at the kitchen table as Joseph did the same. "Caleb, why don't you go outside and see if you can *hilf* with the *kuh*," his father suggested. Without hesitation, Caleb moved toward the back door as Helena gawked after him.

"Is something wrong?" Joseph asked, catching her expression. Helena hesitated, not wanting to interfere.

"By himself?" she asked worriedly. "Does he know the men—or how to handle animals?"

Joseph chuckled, unperturbed. "That's how we do things here," he explained. "He should be working as soon as he gets up. Most *kinner*—er, children, are exposed to farm work from the time they're born."

Warily, she allowed the child to go, but Joseph's confident stance relaxed her slightly. "I guess I'm a little new to how a farm is run."

"You might like it if you give it a chance," Joseph suggested. Helena smiled, but when she met his gaze, she saw that he wasn't smiling back.

"Oh…I don't know if I could manage something like this," she confessed slowly. "I-I have no experience at all."

"You could learn."

Helena settled back in her chair, long fingers trailing over her cold coffee mug now as her mind wandered.

Wasn't I just thinking that for myself? Is this a sign from God?

She suddenly had no idea what to make of the new emotions swelling up inside her as she studied her neighbor. It was completely unfamiliar and contrary to what she was experiencing the day before.

"Are you all right, Helena?" Joseph asked, reading her expression clearly.

"I…" she faltered at the pointed query. "I never got you that coffee."

She rose and busied herself in the kitchen, shaking off the doubts that followed.

I have to sell this place. There are no other options...are there?

Biting on her lower lip, she made up her mind and returned to the table. "Let's discuss business," she said firmly. "How much were you thinking for everything?"

Joseph turned away, and she caught the look of disappointment in his face as he did.

Why does he look crushed? We already talked about this. It's why he's here.

Joseph cleared his throat and sat back at the kitchen table as Helena re-approached with the coffee, reclaiming her seat.

"Have you given any thought to staying here?" he blurted out. "Maybe working the farm yourself?"

The question startled her. "Here? In this house?" she asked slowly.

"I'm sorry. I don't know if you have a *mann*—a husband, or family waiting for you in the city," he mumbled, shooting his eyes downward. "I shouldn't have been presumptuous."

"I don't," she responded, not wanting to give him the wrong idea. "You weren't…but I don't know the first thing about running a farm."

"It can be learned—just like anything else."

She laughed hollowly and waved her arms around. "Frankly, I don't even know how my uncle managed all these years. It seems pretty complicated to me."

"He did it with the help of the community," Joseph explained, dropping his strong forearms back onto the table. "Many of us pitched in to help a single, older *mann* with his needs."

Helena found herself eying his muscular arms, pondering his words carefully.

"But he wasn't Amish," she protested. "Why would you do that?"

"That didn't matter. He did trade with our district and hired men from our community. He spoke *Deutsch* quite well too. Like I said before, Clyde was a *gut mann.*"

"Uncle Clyde?" Helena laughed, amused by the idea of her quiet, slightly crotchety uncle learning anything new at that point of his life.

"He might have converted if he had been a younger *mann,*" Joseph offered. "But I think it was a lot for him to take on at his age."

Helena gaped at him. "Converted?!" she echoed. "As in, become Amish?"

"*Yah,* that's what I mean by convert," Joseph agreed.

"People can do that?!"

"If they learn the *Ordnung* and the language—and are truly committed to *Gott.* It's something that needs to be discussed with the elders, the Deacon, the Bishop and ministers. The community should have a say in the matter as well, but it's rare that anyone is refused if they are truly committed."

She noted the way he looked at her and her heart began to flutter as his intentions began to shine through.

Is he suggesting what I think he is?

It didn't seem real, a girl from the city, coming to the country, to the middle of nowhere to convert into the Amish lifestyle.

He must think I'm something I'm not, Helena thought, shaking her head. And yet Helena suddenly couldn't stop thinking about the appeal of it as she peered into Joseph's earnest blue eyes.

He wants this for me!

"Are you sure you want to sell the land?" Joseph asked again, his tone much softer now. Helen swallowed, considering his words carefully. She had come from Akron so gung-ho, with a plan to be in and out, but now…

The back door opened and Caleb scampered through the kitchen, his face hopeful. "Have you asked her, *Daed?*" the boy demanded. "Is she staying?"

Joseph sprang back in his chair as if he'd been struck, and the conversation suddenly made sense to Helena.

Caleb put him up to this, she realized, shaking her red waves in dismay.

"I-I don't know, *sohn,*" Joseph stuttered uncomfortably. "That is a big decision."

"My *Daed* is a *gut mann,*" Caleb reassured her, spinning to face her earnestly. "He was a *gut mann* to my *Mamm.* He'll be a *gut mann* to you, too. And weddings are fun here."

Helena gasped aloud as she understood what the little boy was expecting, a wife for his father, but Joseph quickly stood, shaking his head vehemently. "Cale, that's enough!"

"It's alright," Helena told them both kindly, feeling no anger toward the boy or his father. Caleb was just a child who had lost his mother, after all. He didn't understand the ways of the world or the nuances of romance.

"We should go," Joseph told his child gruffly, his embarrassment palpable.

"No!" Helena cried. "You just got here. I want you to stay for lunch and we should discuss the amount you have to offer. If I am going to sell this place, I want to have an idea of how much I should be getting."

Joseph and Caleb both hung their heads, but Helena's mind whirled with new possibilities.

Could I keep this place on the side somehow? Still visit if I have someone run it while I live in the city?

But as she snuck glances at the handsome widower and his sad-looking son, she felt a pull that hadn't been there the day before. If she kept the farmhouse, it wouldn't be an income property. She would have to commit to it fully.

The rest of the afternoon passed with a strained awkwardness even though the Lantzes did remain for lunch, which Helena took great pains cooking.

She had looked online for Amish recipes and found what she needed in her uncle's deep freezer to make several of the dishes she had found, impressing her neighbors on her first attempt, despite her nervousness.

"Does it really taste okay?" she asked again when Caleb asked for another helping of chicken pot pie.

"He wouldn't eat it if he didn't like it," Joseph reassured her, also taking another spoonful from his plate. "You're a very *gut* cook."

Helena smiled warmly. "It's been a long time since I've tried my hand in the kitchen," she confessed. "I don't have a lot of time at home."

Joseph frowned at the remark. "If you don't cook, how do you eat?"

"I order in a lot," she admitted. "My work hours keep me at the office late. I do a lot of pizzas and burgers."

Her declaration caused another silence to fall over the dining room table, and she wondered if Joseph was judging her.

"I mean, I wish I had time to cook," she added sheepishly. "But living in the city is expensive."

"One of the *gut* things about running a farm is that everything is here, at your fingertips," Joseph said.

Helena nodded slowly, chalking another point to the idea of running the farm on her own.

He makes it sound so simple, but is it really?

After they ate, Helena cleaned up the dishes and Joseph collected his son, the pair shuffling toward the front door.

"I've given you the numbers if you're still interested in selling," he concluded. "But there's no rush from me. I would like the land to expand my property...but it would also be nice to have you as a neighbor if that interests you, too."

A hot flush tinged Helena's cheeks. "I don't know how that would work, Joe," she mumbled, looking away.

"We could find a way to make it work," he offered firmly, and she wanted to believe him.

"You're a *gut* cook and a nice *frau*," Caleb chirped. "I hope you'll marry my *daed*."

"Caleb!" Joseph frowned softly and Helena giggled.

"Give me some time to think about things," she told Joesph.

"As I said, there's no pressure or rush," he reassured her. "Things are different here than in the city."

Closing the door after seeing them off, Helena leaned against the frame and exhaled, but she barely had time to process the day when her cell began to ring.

With a groan, she pushed herself off the wall and headed into the kitchen, where the device was charging.

"What is going on over there?" Melissa grumbled in her ear when she answered. "You haven't called me all day!"

That's a great question, Helena thought, smothering a sigh.

"I'm still working things out," she replied slowly.

"Is it going to be hard to sell? Is that the problem?"

"No...I don't think so. In fact, I have a buyer already," Helena explained. "But..."

"But what? Helena, work is piling up. You can only do this remote thing for so long, you know. And the bosses aren't going to be understanding forever."

Schedules, deadlines, and pressure are waiting for me back in Akron. Here there's none of that.

"I'm thinking about staying."

The words were out of her mouth before she could think about Melissa's obvious response.

"For how long?" Melissa demanded, not bothering to hide her exasperation.

"Permanently. Did you know that people can convert to being Amish?"

Silence ran so deeply on the other end of the phone, Helena thought she had lost connection with her long-time friend. "Liss?"

"Did you hit your head or something? Are you under duress?" Melissa breathed.

Helena snickered. "No, of course not."

"You're thinking about becoming Amish?!"

"I'm thinking about staying and running the farm. It's really peaceful out here, Liss. You should come and see it—"

"It's a vacation spot at best!" her friend interjected. "It's not a place for a city girl to live. You're an accountant, not a farmer! What the heck do you know about milking cows?"

Helena felt her heart sink. Melissa did make valid points, but she did not want to let go of the idea yet. "I can learn…"

"Learn to be Amish or be a farmer?" Melissa fired back. "What has gotten into you?"

Helena swallowed thickly, her friend's harsh but sensible words making sense. "You're just losing touch with reality because you're away from your life and responsibilities," Melissa went on. "But you have a whole life here—and it's waiting for you."

"You're right," Helena sighed begrudgingly. "I-I don't know what I'm thinking."

"You're not thinking. Tie up whatever you need to tie up there and come home. Honestly, Lena, sometimes I worry about you."

The women said goodbye and Helena replaced the phone on the charger, her eyes trailing toward the wide kitchen widow to take in the brilliant landscape beyond.

She's right. I need to get out of here before I get sucked in by all this...and by Joesph and Caleb.

This was no place for a city girl, no matter how convincing the Lantzes were with their big, blue eyes.

CHAPTER 7

*H*elena did not give a direct answer about the sale of the property over the next week, but Joseph saw her every day. She found some excuse to make her way over from her uncle's house to his farm with a freshly baked pie or casserole, often asking for advice on the cows or the farm hands.

And Joseph was happy to offer every bit of advice he could. Caleb was over the moon to have the pretty new neighbor in sight and visited her house too when Joseph was off working the fields. He would often collect him from Helena's front porch or garden where he would find them planting, the sight filling his heart with pleasure.

But he did not dare ask what her plans were as the weekend approached and Sunday worship neared.

"Daed, will Helena *komme* today?" Caleb asked as they got in their buggy that morning, dawn peeking over the horizon to guide their way across the district toward the Bontrager farm at the other end of the county.

"Where? To the *haus*?" Joseph replied, confused by his son's question.

"*Nee*, to *karrich*," Caleb said, turning his head to stare wide-eyed at his father. Overhead, gray clouds threatened to overtake the morning sky, but the promising rain held off as they moved.

"Oh no, Cale. She is probably going to her own *karrich*…" Joseph trailed off, unsure where Helena spent her Sunday mornings. He had never thought to ask, but he was sure she would not join their sermons. The attempt he had made to suggest a conversion had fallen as flat as a lead balloon.

"Why not?" Caleb whispered, his disappointment piercing Joseph's soul. "Aren't we *gut* enough for her?"

Exhaling, Joseph cast his son a sidelong look, his eyes still fixed on the road ahead.

"Cale, you're too *yung* to understand how the world *warrick*—"

"Stop saying that!" Caleb exploded, folding his arms defiantly over his chest. "I'm not! I'm not a *bobbli*!"

"*Nee*, you're not," Joseph agreed. "But you don't understand the difference between our world and the *Englisch*, not yet."

"Why isn't Danny back if it's so different?" Caleb demanded, his voice cracking. "He's not *cooma* back, is he?"

Joseph's heart lurched again, but he did not want to lie to his son. While he was sure Daniel would eventually return, there was no time limit on his Rumspringa. "Danny will be back," he insisted.

"You don't know that," Caleb muttered and Joseph gnawed on the insides of his cheeks, determined not to argue with his youngest child any more.

He was grateful when they arrived at the Bontragers. Patters of rain fell over the fields and half the district remained outside while the others filtered into the house.

Eli Troyer rushed over to him almost as soon as he arrived. "Did you invite that Englisch *frau* here?"

Immediately, Joseph's head jerked up as he scanned the yard for Helena, knowing exactly who Eli was speaking of. "*Nee*, I didn't."

"She's been spending time with the Deacon," Eli informed him, causing Joseph's breaths to quicken.

"Why?" Joseph demanded, but before Eli could respond, Bishop Hellmann called the service to order and the people inside swarmed out of the farmhouse, toward the pews laid on the grass in the gently drizzling rain.

The women shifted to one side of the property and Joseph moved to the other, with the men, his gaze finally resting on Helena Berry.

He barely recognized her in a simple, modest, homespun dress of blue, covering her entire lithe form.

A lump of pleasure formed in his throat as he tried to wrap his mind around what this could mean.

Is she thinking of staying? Converting?

The last time they had talked, the idea had seemed so farfetched to her, but now, she looked like a proper Amish woman, her face turned forward toward the ministers.

She can't understand any of what's being said!

To his left, someone nudged him. Joseph turned to look at his neighbor from across the road. Luke Schwartz poked his chin at Helena. "Is it true she's an accountant?" he whispered in a tone that was barely audible. Joesph nodded, hardly able to tear his eyes away from Helena as he willed her to look his way.

"Is she staying here, in the county?" Luke asked.

"I don't know," Joesph admitted. "Why?"

Luke shifted uncomfortably and looked nervously at the pulpit to ensure they weren't being overheard before explaining. "I could use some *hilf* with my books if she needs the *warrick*."

As if Helena had heard them speaking about her, she suddenly turned her head, her eyes widening as they locked with Joseph. He offered her a small smile, and she returned it, her cheeks flaming crimson as she turned her head back forward.

"I'll ask her for you," Joseph promised, an idea forming in his mind. He had no idea what Helena's intentions were or if she planned to stay, but she would certainly need money, just like everyone else. Why not put her accounting skills to good use while she decided what she wanted to do?

Caleb was extremely excited to see the young woman after the services were completed and it was almost fifteen minutes before Joseph was able to get Helena alone and ask her what was going on.

"Have you decided to convert?" he asked in disbelief. To his disappointment, she shook her head.

"No…well, I don't know," she bubbled. "I mean…I'm learning about the area, about the Amish. It's not exactly a decision I can take lightly."

"*Nee*, it's not," he conceded with a nod. "I didn't expect to see you here today. I heard you've been meeting with the Deacon, too."

Helena shrugged and looked through the heavying rain, wrapping her hands around her arms. "I-I'm trying to understand what's involved if I were to stay," she admitted. "With being baptized or whatever." She paused to take a breath. "It's a lot."

Joseph tried to hide his sadness at her tone. "It is," he agreed. "But I think it's worth it."

"You must be annoyed with me," Helena told him apologetically. "I've left you hanging on an answer about the property."

His brow knit. "I'm not annoyed in the least. You can take a year if that's what you need to decide. I won't rush you."

A fuzzy smile touched her lips. "I wish my work was as calm as you," she said.

"Speaking of work—I have a *freind* who could use your *hilf* if you're interested."

Her lovely gray eyes popped. "My help?" she repeated. "What help can I possibly offer?"

"Your accounting *hilf*."

They were barely able to speak before they were encompassed by other neighbors and friends, all demanding introductions which Joseph was happy to provide. Helena handled everyone's kindness with a broad smile and pleasantries, but her eyes remained on Joseph as he took Caleb to the sprawling food table to fix a plate and sit, his mind whirling with the possibilities if Helena chose to remain.

When the noonday sun attempted to break through the sooty clouds, half the district filtered out, heading home, and Joseph realized that Helena was walking.

"You can't walk that far!" he declared in shock. "It will take you hours!"

"I got a ride in with the Deacon," she admitted. "But I don't want to bother him now."

She gestured toward the still chattering man, who showed no signs of leaving as Caleb tugged on her hand. "You can *komme* with us!" the boy suggested. "We're right next door!"

Uncertainly, Helena looked at Joseph, who nodded eagerly in agreement. "If I had known you were going to be here today, I would have brought you over."

"Oh…I didn't want to trouble you," she replied gently. "I'm still learning the ways of the community. I had no idea church…*karrich*?" There was a hesitation as Joseph and Caleb laughed, nodding their approval at her Deutsch. "I didn't know it was so far away."

Together, they headed back toward Joseph's buggy, parked on the road, as Caleb told her what Helena must have already known. "We go to a different *haus* every time we have service. This week it's here, but next time, we'll have it somewhere else. Sometimes, we have it at our *haus*, right *Daed?*"

"That's right," Joseph agreed, helping Helena onto the bench.

"And it's only every second week?"

Joseph bobbed his head, opening the back door for Caleb to scamper inside before securing his son in the back and taking the reins in the front. "But we always pray before meals, before bed, whenever we have an opportunity to *denki Gott* for our blessings."

Helena cast him a small smile as he maneuvered the horse cautiously out of the spot, and they headed up the country road. As if God Himself smiled down, a burst of sunshine filtered through the clouds and shone over the damp countryside.

"I've found myself praying a lot more since I've been here," Helena admitted. "Not that I didn't go to church before."

Joseph nodded approvingly. He had suspected that Helena was a godly woman when he had first met her.

"We don't need a *karrich*—a church building to connect with *Gott.*"

"No…I felt very connected to Him today. I'm glad I came." Helena turned her head and stared away from Joseph. He wondered what she was thinking, but he did not press as they rode on silently. Caleb, on the other hand, had no trouble peppering her with questions.

"Will you stay now? If you're *cooma* to *karrich* and dressing like us?"

"Caleb…" Joseph sighed warningly, but Helena put a hand on his arm, shaking her head gently.

"It's all right," she reassured him before swiveling her head back to look at the boy. "I don't know, Caleb. I have been meeting with your elders, the Deacon, and even the Bishop, once. If I were to stay, I have a lot to learn here."

"We can *hilf* you!" Caleb insisted.

"I'm keeping my options open for right now," Helena concluded, but she looked at Joseph when she said this, and his chest tightened.

Luke Schwartz had Helena visit his farm the following Monday, and on Tuesday, she went to the Millers. By Friday, Helena had a full roster of new, independent accounting clients who were delighted to have fresh eyes on their bookkeeping. Helena appeared to relish in the work as she packed up her uncle's house, preparing it for the next stages —whatever it might be.

She had Caleb and Joseph over for supper that evening, and Joseph commented on the boxes piled near the door, a slight nervousness overtaking him at the sight.

"So, you've made up your mind?" he asked slowly after they had a hearty meal of roast chicken and potatoes, a pumpkin pie still sitting in Joseph's stomach as Caleb retreated to the back porch to check on the workers and the livestock.

"What do you mean?" Helena asked, struggling to start the fireplace. Another bout of rain had run through the community all week, leaving a damp chill in the evening air.

"You've packed up so much," Joseph pointed out. "I hope you're still giving me first choice if you're selling."

Helena grunted and struck another match, the head fizzing out as soon as it was lit. Joseph rose from his spot on the sofa and took the box of matches from her as Helena backed away in embarrassment.

"Oh, of course, Joe," she replied, sounding surprised. "I already fired the real estate agent—which, between you and me, was kind of a relief. I wasn't a big fan of that guy, anyway."

Effortlessly, Joseph struck the match and dropped it in the fireplace, the flames catching the newspaper and starting beneath the logs as Helena watched in awe. "How did you do that?"

He shrugged and grinned, setting the screen in front of the hearth. "Practice."

They both sat again, reaching for their hot apple cider, a treat that one of the grateful neighbors had brought over after Helena had straightened out their business accounts. Joesph took a long sip and gestured vaguely toward the pile of boxes. "It looks as though you're packing up the *haus.*"

Caleb re-entered the living room and climbed up on the sofa beside his father.

She won't answer me now that he's here, he thought, stifling his regret, but to his surprise, Helena spoke freely.

"Yes, there are some things that can be donated, clothing that I won't have any use for. Is there a place in Broken Wheel I can send them to help those in need?"

Joseph felt a spark of hope. "I can take them in the *mariye*— tomorrow," he offered. "I have to go into town to get supplies…"

He faltered as he realized something. "The *mannsleit*—the workers. They're still here. I thought you had given them severance."

Helena shrugged and smiled nervously. "I don't know what I'm doing," she replied honestly. "I wake up every morning and I feel so right here but after meeting with the Bishop and Deacon, I don't see how I could ever really become a part of your community, Joe."

"That's not true!" Caleb interjected fiercely. "You're already here!"

She smiled warmly at the impassioned boy. "It's more than just having property here, Caleb. If I were to be a part of your community, really be Amish, I would need to learn Deutsch fluently and the *Ordnung*—"

"Which I could *hilf* you with," Joseph heard himself interrupt her. He pursed his lips together and set his mug down. "If that's what you want."

He heard Helena release a deep breath. "I'm not sure this is a right fit for me," she murmured. "If I'm a right fit for you."

"You are!" Caleb cried out. "*Gott* put you here for a reason! He wouldn't have put me at your door if He didn't want you to stay!"

Joseph inhaled slowly, not wanting to pressure her. "You've made *freind* already and you could continue your business if that's what you want to do, Helena. Maybe you don't want to be a farmer but you will still have a *haus* and the land…"

He met her eyes desperately, hoping she could read his true feelings there, and she met his expression evenly. She bit down on her lower lip, casting her gaze around the living room.

"Don't you like it here, Helena?" Caleb asked meekly.

"I do. More than I ever thought I would," she told the boy honestly. "That's what makes this decision so difficult."

"It doesn't need to be such a difficult decision if you pray on it," Joseph suggested. "We often leave complex matters in *Gott's* hands."

Without a word, Helena took another sip of her cider and nodded as Caleb began to list the attributes of living in the district, but Joseph could see that Helena was not paying the child much mind.

We are asking too much of her and this isn't fair.

"*Komme*, Cale," Joseph said abruptly, rising from his spot.

Helena looked at him in shock. "You're leaving?" she asked.

"You have enough on your plate without us taking up your time," Joseph reminded her stiffly.

She also stood as Caleb complained. "Will we *komme* back in the *mariye*?"

"I think we should give Helena some time to herself to think about what she really wants," Joseph replied. Helena's pretty, gray eyes shadowed at his brusque answer, but she did not argue.

"You can *komme* back anytime you like and help me practice my words, Cale," she suggested weakly. Caleb accepted her answer, even if Joseph remained unconvinced by her commitment. As much as he hoped Helena would stay, he could not hold out hope only to have his heart broken when she decided to go. It was better if he gave her space.

"If you do choose to sell, I'll need some time to get the money together," he reminded her at the door, avoiding her eyes.

"Joe—"

"You know where to find me when you've made up your mind, Helena."

He ushered Caleb out of the house, ignoring the twist in his chest as he felt her eyes boring into him.

"*Daed*, do you think she'll stay?" Caleb asked, excitement pitching his voice.

No, Joseph thought grimly. *I think she's weighed out the pros and cons and will return to the city soon.*

"I don't know," he answered his son, not wanting to drown Caleb in any more disappointment. He had already lost his mother and his brother had been gone for weeks. He did not know what Caleb would do if Helena left, too.

"I think she'll stay," Caleb said as they made their way across the field, toward their house in the distance.

"Why do you say that?"

"Because I've prayed that Helena will be my new *mudder* every night since she got here. *Gott* wouldn't take her away from me, too."

Upset burned at the back of Joseph's throat, but he managed to keep the bitter words from surfacing.

We have to stay away from that frau before she does any more damage to either one of our hearts.

CHAPTER 8

elissa stood at the entrance of the coffee shop, looking around several times, her eyes skipping over her friend until Helena raised her arms dramatically.

"Oh my God!" Melissa gasped, rushing toward her, dropping her oversized designer bag onto the table with a thud. "What are you wearing?!"

Helena glanced down at her simple printed dress, forgetting that she had opted to wear the traditional Amish clothing that day. Her hand subconsciously moved up to touch the base of her neck.

"So, you're Amish now?" Melissa's voice carried throughout the coffee shop and Helena's face stained with humiliation.

"Sit down and lower your voice," she pleaded with her friend. "It's just easier to get the housework done in this than a pantsuit."

Melissa plopped down unceremoniously and glanced around the café, releasing a grunt of frustration. "You could have just come back to the city and grabbed some clothes from your apartment," she reminded Helena. "Assuming you're coming home."

Melissa arched a blonde eyebrow as Helena folded her arms under her chest. An Amish couple entered the restaurant and waved at her across the floor.

"*Hallo*, Helena!" the woman called. "Will we see you at *karrich* on *Sunndaag*?"

"*Yah, yah*," Helena replied, forcing a smile under Melissa's disapproving frown.

"I hope you bring that potato pie you brought last time," the woman said with a chuckle. "My *maedel* insisted I learn how to make some at home."

"I'll get you the recipe," Helena promised, her cheeks flaming. She exhaled as the well-meaning neighbors shuffled toward a booth, leaving Melissa and Helena alone.

"Potato pie? You're making pies now?" Melissa scoffed in disbelief. "You're Suzy freaking Homemaker?"

"I'm trying to blend in here," Helena replied defensively. "And they're *gut* people."

"*Gut people*," Melissa echoed mockingly. "Do you hear yourself? What is going on with you? You're not returning calls from work. You said you'd be back weeks ago, Lena, and now..."

She waved her hand, shaking her head. "I barely know what to say about all this."

"I-I've been trying to figure things out," Helena confessed. "And I think…I think I belong here, in Broken Wheel."

Melissa's full mouth parted into an "O". "Are you having a nervous breakdown or something?"

"No!" Helena fired back, sitting forward to splay her hands over the table.

A server approached the table, but Melissa waved her off. "Give us a minute, please. I might need you to call an ambulance for this one."

"Stop making fun of me, Liss," Helena grumbled. "This past few weeks has been…cathartic. It's so peaceful out here, away from the chaos of the city. There are no deadlines, and people really care about one another."

"Because they don't have a choice!" Melissa retorted. "They have to depend on one another because there's no electricity, no internet. They're sheltered and cut off from reality. Is that really what you want for yourself?"

"That's not true," Helena countered. "It's not like that."

"What is it like, then? You've been gone a month and look at you. You're speaking differently, wearing different clothes, and talking about giving up your entire life, for what?"

An image of Joesph fluttered through Helena's mind, his kind, patient face ever waiting for her response to whether she was staying or going over these past weeks.

Then little Caleb popped through. His bright smile and eager-to-please chirping filtered into her mind, wringing her heart desperately.

"This isn't you, Helena. This isn't your life, no matter how much you've convinced yourself otherwise."

Helena gulped back the stone in her throat, her gaze settling on Melissa's annoyed face. She had called Melissa here to help her attend to her affairs in the city, including packing up her apartment and selling her car.

But now that Melissa was sitting in front of her, addressing all of her previous reservations, all of Helena's doubts came flooding back in a torrent.

"What is it that this life can offer you that you can't find in the city?" Melissa pressed, unwilling to accept her friend's silence. "This isn't like you, Helena, and frankly, I'm worried about you."

"There's a peace here, one that I've never felt in the city. We work together here, and I can still work—"

"As a farmer?" Melissa scoffed.

"As an accountant," Helena muttered, hearing how weak the words sounded aloud now that she was saying them.

"Is that why you called me here? To get my blessing?"

Helena shook her head, dropping her eyes. "No…"

"Well, what then? This is just bizarre. I can't keep covering for you at work and I don't know how much longer you're going to have a job if you keep this up."

More confusion overtook Helena as she nodded, the reality of her actions hitting her abruptly.

"I-I know," she breathed unsteadily. "Y-you're right."

Relief crossed over her friend's face as Melissa reached over the table to squeeze her hand. "Lena, you know I love you, girl. I want you to be happy and if this is really what you want to do, I support it, but it doesn't look like you know what you're doing…do you?"

Miserably, Helena bit on her lower lip.

"Talk to me," Melissa urged. "I can help you if you tell me what's going on."

But how could Helena explain it to her when she wasn't even sure she knew what was happening inside her?

"I-I'm sorry," she whispered, standing. "I shouldn't have made you come all the way down here."

"Lena!" Melissa cried out after her. "Where are you going?!"

But Helena had already hurried out of the café, determined to end this madness once and for all.

Caleb answered the door, his small face lighting up to see Helena standing on the porch.

"Helena!" he cried happily. "Have you *komme* for *nachtesse*?"

Her stomach dropped and she couldn't manage a smile. "Is your *vadder* home, Cale?"

Caleb's smile broadened. "Your *Deutsch* is getting very *gut*!" he announced proudly. "The Bishop is going to have you baptized by next fall, for sure!"

"Where is your father, Caleb?"

His beam faltered at her sharp tone, but he stepped back to allow her inside. "In the *kuche*, making *nachtesse*. We're having *henkel* stew *dienacht*. I'll put an extra bowl out."

"*Nee*—no! I'm not staying, Caleb."

I have to stop that, speaking in Deutsch. I'm not one of them. I'm an Englisher from the city. I don't belong here.

"Caleb?" Joseph's voice traveled out from the kitchen and a moment later, the handsome farmer appeared, wiping his hands. His eyebrows shot up to see Helena stalking toward him. "Helena!"

"I need to talk to you," she told him quietly. "Alone."

Understanding colored Joseph's face, and he turned to his son. "Caleb, go upstairs and wash up for *nachtesse.*"

"I want to stay here with Helena," he whined.

"*Nee!*" both adults said in unison. Joseph paled at her tone.

"Do as you're told, *pliese,*" he insisted. "I need to speak with Helena alone."

Worry wrinkled Caleb's face and Helena crouched down to look at him. "I won't be long, Cale," she promised. "Go do as your...your father says." She exhaled, steeling herself from using any Deutsch words.

Mumbling to himself, Caleb stomped up the stairs, unhappy at being excluded. Ensuring that the little boy was out of earshot, Joseph turned to her. "*Wat* is it? Is everything okay?"

Helena nodded shortly. "I've made a decision," she said without preamble. There was no sense in beating around the bush anymore. She had prolonged the inevitable long enough, living in this fantasy that could not go on, no matter how she tried to spin it.

"A decision about what?" Joseph asked worriedly, his vivid eyes shadowing.

He already knows. He knows what I'm going to say.

"I would like to sell the farm to you if you're still interested," she announced, purposely avoiding his shocked expression.

"*Wat?*" he breathed. "Are you sure?"

"Yes." The word cracked in her throat. "The sooner we can get this done, the better it will be for everyone."

Joseph inadvertently took a step back, his face fraught with shock and disappointment. "If that's really what you want, Helena…"

"It is," she said again. "How long do you think it will take you to get the money together?"

"A week," he replied with just as much flatness.

She nodded. "I'll get the house packed up and deliver it to you empty, then."

Raising her head, she met his eyes, begging him to see how difficult a decision this had been for her, but he merely stared right through her, his upset tangible. "Is there anything else you'll need from me?"

"*Yah,*" Joseph said coldly. "I'll need you to keep your distance from Caleb. You've confused him enough as it is."

Tears welled behind Helena's eyes, but she refused to let Joseph see them.

I deserved that, she realized, nodding as she turned away.

"Understood," she whispered. "Please tell him I said goodbye."

"*Nee,*" Joseph answered coldly. "I think it's better if he just doesn't see you again."

CHAPTER 9

$\mathcal{C}$aleb would not stop asking about Helena over the next few days and Joseph did not know what to tell him. He did not want to lie to his young son, but he also knew when he told Caleb the truth, that Helena was leaving Broken Wheel for good, Caleb's heart would be as shattered as his.

What went so wrong? Why did she decide not to stay when it seemed as if she was leaning toward staying all along?

It had always been a difficult choice, one he could not imagine for himself. His whole life, he had known nothing but the comfort of his community and the peace of his district. But he had also thought that Helena was beginning to understand it, too.

It's not for everyone. It's not for her. I have to accept that.

He did not like the way they had left things, but there was no way he could allow Caleb to spend the last days with Helena. It would only make her leaving worse on him, and Caleb had endured far too much loss already.

All that he could do was collect the money, as he had promised Helena, and pay her on Monday as he had already arranged to take possession of the land and house.

Then he would do his best to move himself and Caleb on without Helena Berry.

Joseph threw himself into work, asking Leah Troyer to keep an eye on his son while he tended to his fields, lest Caleb sneak away to visit Helena when he was not watching.

"The *bu* is asking about Helena an awful lot," the minister's wife commented when he broke for lunch on Friday. "I think he intends to sneak over there."

"Don't let him!" Joseph told her sharply. "It's not a *gut* idea."

Leah eyed him sympathetically. "I thought she would stay," the older woman confessed. "She seemed so excited about joining us and learning our ways."

"She changed her mind," Joseph said shortly. "That's all there is to it."

"She met with an *Englisch freind* at the Sunnyside Café last week. Did you know?"

Joseph shook his head. "It doesn't matter to me," he fibbed.

"I wonder if that *frau* changed her mind."

"Helena is a grown *frau*, capable of making her own decisions," Joseph insisted, unwilling to allow for Leah to get in his mind over reasons and excuses on Helena's behalf. It was true that Helena had become well-liked in the district and that he was not the only one who would be sorry to see her go, but he had wasted enough time waiting on her.

"That doesn't mean that we won't miss her when she's gone. She did wonders with our books at the *bauerie.*"

"Maybe she can arrange to come and visit you," Joseph suggested dully. He secretly hoped she would not make special visits to help the accounting clients she had picked up. The notion of running into her unexpectedly hurt his chest.

"She's leaving?!" Caleb gasped and Joseph cringed, whirling around to confront his small son. "Why didn't you tell me?"

"Cale—" he started to say, but his son was already rushing toward the front door and across the field. "Caleb!"

"Oh dear," Leah sighed from behind Joseph, who lingered on the porch, unsure what to do next. He did not particularly want to chase Caleb onto Helena's property.

"He'll *komme* back after she tells him herself," he reasoned, determined not to face Helena again. "There's *nix* I can do about it now that he knows the truth."

"At least it's not storming *dienacht,*" Leah muttered, pivoting back into the house, and Joseph grimaced, glancing over his shoulder.

Oh Caleb, komme back. There's nix you can say that will make her change her mind. She's gone because she never belonged here in the first place.

Every muscle in Helena's body ached, her neck and back stiff and sore from the endless hours she had spent packing up the house and organizing the contents for Joseph. She had never felt so alone as she had the past five days, a dark cloud descending over her as the impending date drew closer for her to leave.

It's not too late! A small, optimistic voice cried out. *Go to Joseph and tell him that you made a mistake, that you don't want to leave, that you see a future here, with him and Caleb.*

But she had already been down this road with herself and she couldn't do that to the warm-hearted man and his impressionable son who had not come within ten feet of her property since she had agreed to sell the land.

In fact, Helena had not left the farm at all, sure that everyone in town would be judging her and upset for what she'd done.

I just need to get packed and get out of here. Melissa was right. I don't belong here.

The front door opened with a bang and Helena knew who it was even before Caleb's little voice called out accusingly. "You're leaving!"

Drawing in a deep breath, she turned and stalked out of the living room to find him shaking with upset, tears brimming in his lovely, azure eyes. "Oh, Caleb—"

"You didn't *komme* and say goodbye!"

"Your father and I thought it was better if I left without saying goodbye," she explained quickly, not wanting to cause him more pain. Slowly, she crouched down in front of him. "Please, Caleb, don't be upset."

"You promised to stay!" he sobbed, allowing the tears to fall freely now and shame choked Helena.

Her chin dropped. "No, Caleb, that's not true." She sighed, extending her arms toward him. "I couldn't promise that because I never knew if I could stay."

"Why not? Why can't you stay? I'll be *gut*! I won't be any trouble!"

"Oh, *liebling...*" Helena embraced him tightly, feeling his small body quake against her. "It's not about you, Caleb. It's not your fault."

"Why does everyone leave?" Caleb bawled. "What did I do?"

"*Nee, nee*, Caleb," she whispered, rocking him as shame overwhelmed her. "This is not about you."

Sniffling, Caleb's head fell back, and he looked accusingly at her. "You said you would stay!" he insisted.

"Caleb, I don't fit in here," Helena started to say, but the boy wouldn't listen. He wriggled out of her hold and folded his arms over his chest.

"Then why did you take so long to decide?"

He has a good point. I shouldn't have drawn it out as long as I did. That wasn't fair to anyone.

"You deserve a *gut Amisch mudder* and your *vadder* deserves a *gut Amisch weib*," she explained to him.

"You can be her!"

"*Wat* is all this shouting about?"

Helena straightened up as the little boy spun around. Even before Caleb called out his name, she knew who it was, standing at the threshold of the doorway, Joseph awkwardly behind him. The brilliant blue of the young man's eyes was a giveaway to his relationship with the father and son.

"Danny!" Caleb almost screamed, rushing toward his older brother.

"I-I'm sorry, Helena," Joseph said sheepishly. "He insisted on seeing Caleb when I told him what happened."

The brothers embraced, but Helena was unbothered by the reunion. She hoped that Daniel would show Caleb how bad a fit she was to the community.

Daniel hugged his younger sibling, but his eyes were on Helena, a gentle smile on his lips. His resemblance to Joseph stole her breath.

"I don't mean to be a bother, Helena, but could I trouble you for a glass of water? I've been traveling all day."

Helena nodded nervously and turned to get him one, unsure of what else to do now that all the Lantzes were gathered in her uncle's foyer.

She hesitated between the kitchen and hallway. "Did you want to come and sit down for a bit?" she offered on a whim.

"*Yah*, Danny, *komme* and sit," Caleb decided for him, leading his older sibling into the house. Joseph remained at the doorway, but Helena waved him through.

"There's no sense in you standing there," she told the man. Gratefully, Joseph shuffled across the threshold, offering her a sheepish look.

"I tried to have him wait until Caleb came *deheem*," he said quietly. "But he wanted to see him right away, particularly when I told him how missed he was."

"It's all right. I'm glad they're reunited now. It wasn't my idea for you to stay away, if you recall."

Shame replaced his embarrassment but Joseph said nothing, following her through the hall and into the kitchen where she found the boys iced tea instead of the water that Daniel had requested.

"You were gone so long!" Caleb complained. "I didn't think you'd *komme* back!"

Daniel chuckled, flopping onto one of the chairs. "Are you kidding? Did you really think I'd leave you behind?"

"*Mamm* did," Caleb reminded him, and Daniel's smile faded.

"*Mamm* was very *grank*, Cale. I was only on Rumspringa. There was never any doubt about my faith, was there?"

He nodded appreciatively as Helena set the glasses down and took a big swig, confirming the thirst he had claimed earlier before speaking again. "I would have been back sooner but my *freind* wanted to stay longer."

"You should have come *deheem*!" Caleb pouted. "Maybe you could have convinced Helena to stay!"

Daniel straightened himself in his chair and offered Helena a warm smile. "I heard that you helped my *bruder* the *nacht* of the storm," he said.

"She's helped the whole community with their books too," Joseph offered, pride tinging his voice, but it was laced with a sadness that Helena could not ignore.

"It sounds like you've been a fine addition to Broken Wheel," Daniel offered. "I'm sorry I won't get to know you better."

Helena blushed.

He gets his charms from his father, I see.

"I-I have a whole life in the city," she mumbled, toying with her fingers. "I've been gone too long already."

"*Yah*, I know what you mean," Daniel agreed. "I felt the same way when I was in Akron."

Her head jerked up. "You were in Akron?" She hadn't realized that.

"Oh, *yah*. You didn't know?"

She shook her head.

"*Yah*, I can see the appeal," he went on, never losing his charming smile, even as his father and brother became more dismayed. "There is never any loss for things to do. But the people are much ruder, aren't they?"

Helena thought of Melissa and the way she had brusquely brushed off her desire to stay in Broken Wheel.

"There's no real sense of *familye*…or *Gott*, despite the churches."

Her mind trailed back to the first worship she had attended, how close to God she had felt, possibly for the first time in her life.

"I couldn't live anywhere but here," Daniel concluded, ruffling his brother's hair. "But I have never known anything else."

"I want this too!" Helena wheezed, her heart squeezing in her chest.

"Helena!" Joseph said sharply, his face paling as Caleb's expression grew excited. She hung her head, the confusion and conflict that had been waging inside her finally falling into place as Daniel's words settled inside her.

"Can I talk to you for a minute?" Joseph asked gruffly, spinning toward the front of the house. He did not sound pleased, but Helena didn't blame him.

Swallowing, she followed him, knowing exactly what he was going to say before he opened his mouth.

"Helena—"

"I know!" she interrupted him. "I've been back and forth, back and forth. But this...this is what I want."

"You're confusing Caleb!" His face was drawn, serious and distinctly upset. "You can't keep changing your mind."

"I haven't been fair to you or Caleb," she agreed. "But I also haven't been fair to myself."

Joseph cocked his head and peered pensively at her, waiting for Helena to elaborate on her statement but she collected her thoughts silently for a long moment, ensuring that she wanted this, truly wanted what she was about to say.

"Daniel was right. The city has a lot to offer," she finally went on. "It has housed me my whole life...but it's not home. My Uncle Clyde, he found home here, in this community, even if he never did convert. I-I found a lot of indications that he wanted to when I was packing up his belongings."

"He was a *gut mann,* a *mann* of *Gott.*"

Helena exhaled. "I wish I'd known him better. Maybe he left me this *haus* because he saw something in me that reminded me of himself? I don't know, and I'll never really know, but the more time I spend here, the more I realize that I can't just walk away."

"You've said this before," Joseph cautioned. "And you can't keep breaking Caleb's heart."

Helena reached for his hands. "Is it only Caleb's heart that you're worried about?" she asked huskily, her shoulders stiffening as she expected him to withdraw. Too many times she had given him false hope over these past weeks and now, he refused to meet her steadfast gaze.

"I think I've made my position on the matter clear, Helena..." he mumbled.

"I want to stay," she said firmly. "I mean it, Joe. I'm not going anywhere—as long as you'll have me."

Exhaling, he raised his head and locked eyes with her, the shadow of doubt lifting as he read the sincerity in her earnest, gray eyes.

"Are you sure this time?"

"*Yah*, I'm sure," she promised. "I will work hard and become fluent in *Deutsch*. I will take all the classes with the Deacon and learn the Ordnung, front to back—"

His hands tightened on hers and relief swept through her as she recognized that he believed her.

"I will *hilf* you—*Gott* willing."

"*Gott* has already shown his intentions," Helena murmured, stepping closer to tilt her head toward the man sweetly. "He has wanted me to be here all along, just like Caleb said."

"I knew it!" Caleb squealed, forcing them apart with a small laugh. The boy hopped from one foot to another as he stared at Helena and his father, a huge beam overtaking his face. "I prayed for this!"

"*Komme*, Cale." Daniel chuckled, steering his brother back into the kitchen with an apologetic smile, but Helena was not embarrassed.

Denki Gott, she thought silently as Joseph followed his sons into the other room, her heart fluttering with happiness. *Denki for giving me such a patient, kind mann. I won't disappoint him, or Caleb, again.*

Outside, thunder rumbled in the distance as if God had answered her, and Helena's eyes opened again. It was as if her time in Broken Wheel was about to come full circle to a proper close.

EPILOGUE

TWO YEARS LATER...

The wail of a baby interrupted the very end of the ceremony and May quickly swaddled her newborn daughter tightly as Daniel looked across from the men's section worriedly toward his wife. But Helena barely noticed her stepson's discomfort as she stared into the eyes of her husband, their vows to one another confirmed before the district finally.

"*Pliese,* hang your head in prayer," the bishop instructed. Helena's heart flittered, knowing that this was the last of the prayers before the reception would commence, but Baby Abigail's screams pierced through the autumn day, interrupting the silence and cutting the moment short.

"*Aamen,*" the Bishop said with a sigh, sounding vaguely irritated. Helena beamed at her husband and Joseph smiled back, the men and women rising from their respective seats to mingle along the Lantz's joint property.

"I can't believe you're married!" Melissa cooed, joining her side before Helena could utter a single word to anyone else. "You actually went through with all of this!"

Helena rolled her eyes and eyed her friend, impressed at the modest dress that Melissa had selected for the event. She had only ever been to the farm twice since Helena had announced that she was staying.

"I'm in love," Helena answered simply, watching Joseph join his sons with the ministers. But his intense blue eyes remained on her face, casting a warmth over her as she spoke with her English friend.

"Everyone is really nice," Melissa confessed in a low voice, glancing around at the other guests.

Helena laughed. "Of course they are. This is a wedding, Liss."

"I know, but I'm not one of them and you know how the Amish are..." she trailed off when she caught Helena's reproving look.

"*Yah*, I do know how the *Amisch* are," she replied quietly. "They're warm and loving, accepting and kind. And they are amazing cooks. Go get yourself something to *esse*."

Embarrassed, Melissa nodded. "I don't think I'll ever get used to you talking like that," she muttered, heading toward the long, prettily dressed tables under the pine trees nearby.

A fresh, cool breeze wafted through the field, tousling the hair of children playing nearby, Caleb among them. He grinned up at his stepmother, his face filling out nicely for a boy of seven.

He's going to be as handsome as his vadder, Helena thought affectionately.

"Abby ruined the ceremony," he complained.

"She did not." Helena frowned at him. "She's a *bobbli*. *Bobbli* will cry. That's what they do."

"I didn't cry like that when I was a *boppli*," he argued.

"Oh *yah*, you did," Joseph countered, joining his new wife and youngest son. "You never stopped crying. Your poor *mudder* never got any sleep at all."

The trio fell silent at the mention of Miriam, their heads bowing respectfully at her memory.

"*Yah*, that's right," Daniel agreed, stepping up to his family. "I would take you out in the wooden *waegel* and bounce you around until you fell asleep." As if a light illuminated in his eye, he looked toward his wife, holding up a finger. "One minute, I'll be right back!"

Joseph chuckled. "That's a *gut* trick for crying *bobbli*," he told Helena. "The movement puts them right to sleep."

"Like car rides," Helena said without thinking. All eyes fell on her and she flushed as they laughed. "*Es dutt mer leed*. It will take some time before I forget all about my *auld* life."

Joseph took her hand as Caleb was whisked off by one of his friends, the new couple now on their own again.

"No one wants you to forget your old life, *liebling*," he promised. "I only want you to look to the future with us, in your new life."

They began to walk through the throng of people, Helena's heart swelling in appreciation at the turn out for the day. It seemed that the whole community had come to celebrate their highly anticipated wedding, taking place only three weeks after Helena's baptism.

She had been willing to wait until the following year for the wedding, but it had been Caleb who had begged for his father and Helena to marry before the first snow fell so that they could all live under the same roof for Christmas. He did not want another holiday season without a mother figure.

The bishop and deacon had been reluctant but after conferring with the ministers, everyone had agreed that Helena had worked very hard over the past two years with her studies and prayers, deeming her worthy of both the baptism and the wedding, even if the situation was not typical.

"May will be happy to be moving into the house," Helena commented, pausing on the edge of the property to look far across the field toward her inherited home. The building was nothing more than an outline from here, but she was sure Daniel and his wife had already begun moving their belongings to the property earlier in the day as she had readied herself for the ceremony.

"It will be nice to have a good night's sleep without a screaming *bobbli* keeping us up all *nacht* too," Joseph teased.

Helena peered at him through her peripheral vision. "Will you say the same thing about our *kinner*?"

He balked, then smiled, as if he had not considered that they would soon be announcing their own good news to Daniel and Caleb—another sibling for them to cherish.

"Of course not. Our *bobbli* will be a perfect *engel*," he joked, brushing a kiss over her cheek. Helena's eyes closed, and she inhaled deeply, relishing the deep sense of peace that stole over her. Daniel, May, and Abigail would move into Clyde's house, now removed of electricity and modern gadgets. After their short honeymoon to the far end of Holmes County,

Helena would return to move in with Joseph and Caleb in their sprawling ranch house, both properties combined now.

She wondered if her Uncle Clyde would be happy with the way his land had been distributed, if she had done well by his memory.

"*Komme, weib*," Joseph said gently, sensing her drifting off into a melancholic reverie. "Our guests await us."

"Lead the way, *mann*," she agreed, smiling brightly. "I will follow you anywhere."

~*~*~

I do hope that you enjoyed reading my story.

May I suggest that you might also like to read my '*Amish Love and Faith Collection*' - *24 Book Box Set* that readers are loving!

Available on Amazon for just $0.99 or Free with Kindle Unlimited simply by clicking on the link below.

Click here to get your copy of 'Amish Love and Faith Collection - 24 Book Box Set' - Today!

Sample of Chapter One

Cora giggled and pinned Linda's tresses up higher, the blonde curls falling haphazardly over the younger girl's face. The feeling of the *Englischer* touching her hair was slightly unnerving but Linda didn't pull away. She was slowly learning to tolerate the brash girl, although with much less gusto than her other Amish friends.

"What about this?" her new friend asked, laughing. "Is this how they wear their hair in Amish country?"

Linda swatted the brunette away playfully, her blue eyes alight with laughter. It was moderately amusing how little the *Englisch* knew about their way of life.

"I already told you that we wear our hair in braids most of the time, underneath our caps," Linda replied, turning back to look at herself in the mirror. "You ask so many questions about my home. It's not all that exciting."

"Please!" Cora laughed. "It's not every day I get to meet a real-life pack of Amish kids. You bet your ass I'm going to ask all the questions I want."

Linda flushed at Cora's free speech, the color tinging her cheeks well enough for the other girl to notice.

"And look at you! Turning red just because I cussed!" Cora howled. "How are you guys still in existence in this day and age?"

Cora guffawed as something occurred to her.

"Oh, they are going to love you tonight!"

Linda blinked and looked at the girl curiously.

"Tonight?" she echoed. "What's tonight?"

Cora glanced toward the hallway where the voices of the others could be heard talking and laughing in the living room. Leah was always the loudest, demanding that the channel be changed on the television. Linda wished Cora would go back out there with the others and let her read in peace.

"Didn't Mark tell you? We're going to a party tonight," Cora explained. Linda shifted uncomfortably in her seat, maintaining her wan smile but the thought made her nervous.

Is there ever a night when some kind of social event isn't happening?

It wasn't that Linda was opposed to gatherings. She simply did not like the way the English passed their time.

"What kind of party?" she asked. Cora shrugged and flopped onto the bed.

"It's just a bunch of kids from school. Drake's dad's out of town and he always has huge bashes when he can. It's gonna be wild! You'll have a great time."

"Oh."

Uncertainly, Linda met Cora's gaze in the mirror.

"Oh what?" Cora demanded, sounding annoyed.

"I-I don't know…" Linda continued slowly. Cora grunted.

"The others are right about you," she complained, her voice rising an octave as she folded her arms over her ample bosom. "You are boring."

Linda's smile faded away, a twinge of hurt shooting through her. She knew she shouldn't care what the others thought about her because she didn't want to drink, smoke cigarettes or whatever was in that foul-smelling burning paper they passed around. Being Amish was not a popularity contest but during *rumspringa*, Linda was learning that all the rules from home were out the window and she couldn't deny that the words hurt.

"Who said that I'm boring?" she wondered before she could stop herself. Cora shrugged again.

"I don't know. Someone said they couldn't believe you'd even come to Philly for your... what's it called again?"

"Rumspringa?"

"Right," Cora went on. "They thought you wouldn't be brave enough to do the trip."

Every word Cora spoke drove another needle of upset into Linda's heart. It was true that she had not wanted to take the trip into the city but her mother had been worried about Linda's cousin, Leah.

"You must go and keep an eye on her, *lieb*," Hannah Schwartz begged her youngest daughter. "Leah's judgement is not as good as yours. You being there will keep her from forgetting where she comes from."

"But *Mamm*, the point of *rumspringa* is for her to find herself," Linda had complained. In the end, Hannah had appealed to Linda's guilt and there she was on a trip she could have done without.

"Anyway, I'm not surprised that you're bailing," Cora went on, jumping up from the bed. "Your cousin said you probably wouldn't want to come. I guess it'll just be more fun for us while you sit around here being boring."

Linda chewed on the insides of her cheeks as she pondered on Cora's words.

I don't want to go to a party with a bunch of Englisch drinking and swearing, she thought. *But I did come here to watch over Leah. If something happens to her and I'm not there...*

She shuddered to think about it.

"*Nee*, I'm coming," she said as Cora ambled toward the door. The brunette paused, a slow smile creeping over her face.

"Yeah?" she asked. Linda forced a beam and nodded quickly.

"*Yah*, for sure."

Cora squealed and clapped her hands, rushing to give Linda an unsolicited hug, again making her tense.

"You're going to have so much fun," Cora promised, turning back to rifle through Linda's trunk that was already open on the bed. "Let's see if you have anything suitable to wear. Drake is going to love you! I told him all about you guys and he really likes blondes."

She winked meaningfully at Linda who turned her head away before Cora could see her blush again.

That's just what I need, Linda thought dryly. *A romance with an Englischer.*

But she did not speak her thoughts aloud. In two days they would be returning to the district where she could resume her quiet life without four roommates and their incessant desire to corrupt themselves in every possible way. In another month, she would be baptized and then the only interaction she would have with English teenagers would be when she was at the market.

It will be fun, Linda told herself as she studied her face in the glass as Cora continued to chatter behind her. *When will I ever get another opportunity to attend an event like this?*

Yet, even then, she could not suppress the inexplicable feeling of dread rising in her gut, as if God was trying to warn her away from whatever the night held.

. . .

Click here to get your copy of 'Amish Love and Faith Collection - 24 Book Box Set' - Today!

A NOTE FROM THE AUTHOR

Dear Reader,

I do hope that you enjoyed reading '**For the Sake of His Beloved Daughter**'

Possibly you even identify with the characters in some small way. Many of us presume to know God's will for our lives, and don't realize that His timing often does not match our own.

The foremost reason that I love writing about the Amish is that their lifestyle is diametrically opposed to the Western norm. The simplicity and purity evident there is so vastly refreshing that the story lines derived from them are suitable for everyone.

Be sure to keep an eye out for the next book which is coming soon.

Emma Cartwright

Thank You!

Thank you for purchasing this book. We hope that you have enjoyed reading it.

If you enjoyed reading this book **please may you consider leaving a review** — it really would help greatly to get the word out!

~

Newsletter

If you love reading sweet, clean, Amish Romance stories why not join Emma Cartwright's newsletter and receive advance notification of new releases and more!

Simply sign up here: http://eepurl.com/dgw2I5

And get your *FREE* copy of **Amish Unexpected Love**

Contact Me

If you'd simply like to drop us a line you can contact us at **emma@emmacartwrightauthor.com**

You can also connect with me on my new **Facebook page.**

I will always let you know about new releases on my Facebook page, so it is worth liking that if you get the chance.

LIKE EMMA'S FB PAGE HERE

I welcome your thoughts and would love to hear from you!

I will then also be able to let you know about new books coming out along with Amazon special deals etc

Manufactured by Amazon.ca
Acheson, AB

15618239R00057